UKRAINE SKIES, BALTIMORE LIGHTS

PETE GODSTON

Peter Phillips Godston

Second Edition (June 2017)

ISBN-13: 978-1541347786 ISBN-10: 1541347781

Fiction > General > Action and Adventure

To my daughters,

In the hope that I may someday inspire them to the extent that they inspire me.

TABLE OF CONTENTS

Cleo

What a blessing, we are born as babies. We are perplexed in a totally new environment. A very dangerous environment. Helpless little babies can't run off and get themselves into trouble, can they? Our mothers' bodies have an allergic reaction (finally!) and out we come. Well, perhaps it isn't simple as that (ask any mother). Except in the early 1700's, in a cave in Ukraine, a woman was born fully into adulthood.

It was dark. Very dark. Candles flickering, making everything appear a bit brown. "My God," (Bozhe Moy, to be precise) one of them had said, "She isn't wrapped. Aren't they always wrapped?" The other man had responded, "How long has she been here? Supposedly hundreds of years? But this girl must have been buried a few weeks ago."

"Someone has played a prank on us," said the first man, before she opened her eyes. When she did that, however, both men went silent and their eyes appeared to grow an extra size.

"You two should just shut up." She understood what they said and had words to say to them, although you might have selected other words in this case. Perhaps, "Good afternoon," or "It's so wonderful to meet you." But this full-grown baby was already frustrated with the bumbling birthers so she impolitely asked them to stop talking. Then she sat up.

The two men shuffled rapidly backwards, one tripping and falling, the other scrambling to the opposite side of the cave. She put her hands on the side of the box, gazing at the box, the multiple layers, at her simple linen clothing, then she turned and looked at the man at the opposite side of the cave.

The man who had fallen was slithering away. She didn't anticipate needing to deal with him at all. But this other man, the one with the torch, she would need to deal with him. She jumped to his side and gripped his neck, pinning the hand with the torch to the wall.

"What are you doing, disturbing my sleep?" she asked him. He tried to knock her hand away from his neck, but of course, he was unable to break her grip. He coughed, managing to say "the Tsar." She released him. "the Tsar?" she asked. "Yes, the Tsar wanted ground mummy. They say it has.." the man paused, wondering what his colleague was up to, finding him in the shadows and feeling assured when he saw the crow bar (or what passed for a crow bar in those days).

"umm.. medicinal powers." he finished. Okay, that was silly. Around the turn of the Eighteenth century people did really think that ground mummy had medicinal powers. For centuries the very existence of mummies was beyond the awareness of everyone. Then beyond the awareness of all but the most educated. Very educated, in some spots badly educated (medicinal powers? Really?). In any event, this flunky from Tsar Peter the Great's court probably believed it, and this instant, gripped by someone alive, not a mummy, he hoped the woman choking him hadn't followed his glance, because he was frightened. His colleague had a crow bar, but how effective would that clumsy oaf be swinging that? Also, this woman had jumped from her box to his side, a jump spanning the cave, and seized his neck in a grip he wasn't able to break.

"Where is this Tsar?" she asked him, a moment before the crow bar bounced off her head. She turning to his colleague, annoyed.

She took a step toward her attacker, caught his arm under the elbow and drove her other hand into his chest. She tossed this second man aside then returned to the first.

"Tell me the full name of this Tsar and where I might find him." After he stumbled through those words, Cleo crushed his head against the wall of the cave and walked out. To find the Tsar, of course.

Outside the crypt she saw the glowing orbs. She ignored them, walking down the steep hill across rocks and rubble, but they followed her. When she bent to pick up a rock, they hesitated, those glowing orbs.

She considered a well-pitched throw at her "tail," but thought the better of that option and dropped the rock. Instead she picked up a stick and threw it down the hill. The orbs bounced down the precipice, following the stick, and she bounced down along the pattern the creature had chosen.

When her new red dog produced the stick, she took it from his mouth. It licked the juices from her hand and she tossed the stick again. Perhaps a companion wouldn't be a bad thing.

##

"We are cat people, not dog people."

Cleo was surprised to find a beautiful middle aged woman sitting on a bench in the barn she selected. She squinted at the woman and turned to her red dog. "Sadites," she told him. He sat dutifully at her side.

"You don't remember me?" the woman asked.

"Have we met?" Cleo asked. What was this strange language… and how can she understand and speak it?

"Of course not," muttered ISIS, with a smirk. "Well, there was a time I was your goddess and you, young princess, were the apple of Ra's eye. Then of course you ran off with that Julius fellow, scandalizing all of Rome."

"Your glorious country has been struggling ever since. I might add that the author will receive quite a pile of manure for this Deux ex Machina, but who better to play that role here than yours truly?"

"At risk of adding several wheelbarrows to the criticism, I'm going to give you some advice. You have learned how to find Tsar Peter. I suggest you attend the unification party at the edges of town tomorrow, and learn about this Swedish Charles XII. Learn how to shoot one of those clumsy flintlocks... and refresh your memory of a blade. They've gotten quite nice since you handled one." Isis handed Cleo a dagger in its leather and gold trimmed sheath. The sun god symbolism at the end of the handle appeared strangely familiar to Cleo.

"Once you have promised the Tsar you will kill his Swedish rival, find the Danish king. He evidently enjoys masquerade balls, where perhaps you might offer to dispense with the Swede in return for a ship to America."

Cleo was confused. "You don't understand this yet, but you will catch on. You always do." Isis considered disappearing with a flash, in a cloud of smoke, but instead turned to walk away.

"Oh," she said, as an afterthought. "Get rid of the dog." Then, tossing Cleo a coin of the local realm, said "Get yourself a room. There is a vacancy at the inn for you."

"Thank you," called Cleo, scratching Wolf behind the ears. "But I think I will keep you," she whispered to her new companion. "I heard that," shouted ISIS.

##

Isis offered her gloved hand to the carriage driver, who ushered her to the inside of a well-appointed cabin on wheels. "Really, these vehicles are so clumsy compared to magic. But, I suppose, helpful for understanding the trials of my little princess."

Squeaking, bouncing travel, complete with snorting horses and dirty faced peasants who stared, mostly without emotion, but an occasional stain of jealousy upon a face. "Let them eat cake," thought ISIS.

She didn't notice Taigen Sessai on a horse as her carriage rode past. Like a candle burning in a window? Sessai had never met Isis, although he was aware of the ancient Egyptian mythology regarding her existence. No samurai would ever have guessed that Cleo had an ally in this century, much less one with the resume of a retired goddess.

Indeed, no one in the Danish court knew who ISIS was either. They thought she was some exotic overthrown queen. What government was it she claimed? It didn't matter. Her knowledge was helpful, and the

Reventflows enjoyed having her around—even engaged her privateer regarding St Thomas. How would she orchestrate an easy access for Cleo? More importantly, how to insure Cleo has no idea it happened. Yes, children can be so willful when parents try to help. "Oh, the tortures of a retired goddess," thought ISIS. "More Deux ex Machina," thought her active and creative mind.

##

"You be good," Cleo told the red dog, as she left for the celebration. Mead, meats, even apples were there for the taking. The barn was hot, jammed with peasants and petty nobility alike. Three men were dancing the Ukrainian classic, butts low to the ground, heels kicking out. Cleo hovered near a circle of teenage girls admiring the dancers.

"Stefan… Stefan… Stefan," she kept hearing, "the champion of East Bank," finally deducing he was the middle dancer, a warrior and still without a wife. They ended that song, the three men clutched hands, exchanged bear hugs and found mead mugs. Girls and other soldiers sought him, she asked questions of anyone willing.

"Yes, well," said a man, when she asked if things went well on the battlefield. "We don't like Peter the Great anymore," said a woman. "The Swedes are famous allies," said another.

Finally, she found herself close to Stefan during a breath break. "So you are the Champion of East Bank?" she asked. He grabbed her by the waist, twirled her around and lifted her into the air.

"Konyechna," he said in his tongue, smiling into her glittering eyes. "Another Julius," she wondered, after he set her down and bounced to the next conversation.

There was more that evening, but more on that later. Cleo left the next morning for Saint

Petersburg, where the Tsar was rumored to be staying with his secret queen.

##

A petty nobleman evidently thought he might take advantage when he saw what appeared to be a young woman walking her dog near the Dnipr River. He dismounted.

"It is a cold day for a walk," said the man.

"Safer to walk, then ride," answered Cleo.

"Ah, but if you consent to a ride, I will have a present for you," smiled the nobleman.

"I won't need presents, man."

Her reply angered him. "If you don't watch your attitude, you may meet both my swords, flesh and steel," he said, drawing his sword.

In a moment, Cleo stepped into his space, removing her dagger from her petticoat faster than even Wolf would have reacted. She gazed into the nobleman's grey eyes, pulling him to her with her hilt, thrust into the center of his back. "If you wish to introduce me to your two swords, you have to be quicker."

The noble's jaw dropped, and his sword clattered on the cobblestones. She removed the dagger from his back and wiped it on his trousers. Then she took a boot in one hand, a glove in the other, and with a spin, launched the body to the center of the Dnipr.

She watched him float downstream, slowly sinking, then picked up his sword, examining her new weapon. She mounted her new horse and called to Wolf. "Let's go," she said.

##

"May I try?" she asked the men, engaging targets with flintlocks. "These bullets are expensive," said one.

"Aw, let the boy try. Perhaps he will join us." Six men exchanged knowing laughs. They think I won't have a choice, thought Cleo.

There was a delay between the trigger pull and a small explosion near her ear. She was able to hold that aiming point to the spot. "Not bad," said the sergeant.

So, Cleo, dressed like a Russian soldier, was on the line with a flintlock when Peter the Great came to review. "Who will hit the vulture?"

At twice the distance from the targets, 100 yards high in a tree, sat a vulture on a branch. Cleo adjusted her aim and called "Delal." Confidence, as if she were a boy.

The vulture fell from the tree. Upon examination, it was missing its head. Peter the Great handed Cleo a coin. "Find me after Poltava. We might have a need for you." She smiled.

##

So instead of resting for eternity in a Kievan cave, Cleo found herself walking next to Peter the Great on the fields at Poltava. Evidently she considered it a debt to him, that he should have requested ground mummy and inadvertently broken into her sleep, freed her from that little box and let her back into the world to promulgate her mischief. Of course he had no idea she was the ground mummy they had been sent to find, only that the two fools he sent were found dead in the cave. He assumed logically that they had been killed by robbers, who took the mummy and sold its ground treasure somewhere else in Europe.

Her red dog trotted at a distance, examining carcasses and pockets, occasionally pulling at something. She ignored the dog and focused on her prospective customer.

On this day Peter the Great only knew that he was talking with a female assassin, who had gained a reputation for her knife work and expertise with a flintlock, already in their brief acquaintance.

Peter turned to her. "The son of a bitch got away. I have massacred pretty much everyone, but the son of a bitch got away, with Mazeppa." She gazed at the many bodies, already rotting on the field. "What of the two body guards. I wish to know about them."

He scoffed. "They are nothing. If you take him with a flintlock, they cannot interfere." She pondered his reply as they walked among the cadavers, thinking "they are something to me." Instead she asked, "What of this Mazeppa? You don't want me to take him?"

Peter frowned. "No, Mazeppa is an old, broken man. He won't live long. It is Charles that I want. That son of a bitch has been an unexpected thorn in my side."

Cleo frowned. "In any event, you aren't paying me enough. You have cut the previous assassin in half after reclaiming your advance. I want double."

Peter pondered her request, turning to her with a small smile on his face. He twisted his mustache. "It is a great problem to fail the Tsar. Surely you understand."

"Your Highness," she replied, "that assassin didn't fail you. The shot he made a few days ago, truly remarkable. He just didn't understand gravity."

"Gravity?" Peter asked. She turned to him and replied, "Charles is well protected. No one can get close. Your shooter was a several hectares away and still hit the man in his ankle. Your assassin had the line precisely right, but he didn't understand the bullet drop." She turned away. "incredible shot," she mumbled again.

"Hmm," Peter replied, handing her a small but heavy purse. "Double it is. I expected you to ask for three." She shook the purse up and down. "Do not fail me. I will find you if you do," he added, then walked away.

"And what do you think you will do, if you should find me," she thought to herself. She quietly walked back to her horse, mounted, and rode off.

##

She glanced at the dog. They smelled nothing. Her quarry had passed too long ago. Quickly she assessed the two body guards would have gone with Mazeppa, and not with Charles. "Charles can wait," she decided. Then she climbed on her horse and spurred him down the southeast fork.

The road to Bendery wasn't an easy one in those days. Heading south, with a flintlock and sword, she might easily have been mistaken for a wealthy merchant or, worse yet, thief. Someone who found the purse from Peter would have certainly been delighted.

Along the way, she thought about the challenge of taking Charles. Her pride suggested the same method, and the same distance, as the previous assassin. She placed her hand on the leather casing around the flintlock. But her attention was commanded, two mounted ruffians were on the road, in her way.

"Zdrast, Gospozha," she had said in her deepest guttural voice. "Mozhna proity?" One replied, in

Russian, "There is a toll," glancing sideways at his colleague in the method thieves and ruffians have shared through the centuries. "Ahh," responded Cleo. She spurred her horse, cutting the speaking man in half with her sword. The dog leapt at the companion, then her sword sent that man's head to another location. Spurring her horse to a gallop, she glanced at the dog, wondering if he would keep up.

After thirty minutes, she thought a slower pace would be better for her horse.

She chose to ride through the night, that night, but stopped in an inn, halfway through the next day. In exchange for a gold coin, the innkeeper was happy to give her a nice room all to herself, with a bath, on the second floor. She left the dog to fend for himself.

Later that evening, feeling more refreshed than any day since the days in the Tsar's court, she enjoyed a meal and mead under the innkeeper's hospitality. Two men were talking about a killing on the road to Kiev. They were glancing at her.

She discretely touched the dagger under her cape, for her benefit, unseen by others there that day. She smiled and knew no one would confront her. Several days later, Cleo arrived at Bendery.

She doubled back, hiding both the flintlock and sword near the top of a forested hill. "Perhaps I will come back for them," she thought. Then she rode back to the fortress and asked to see the Sergeant of the Guard. "We always have room for an enlisted man," said the sergeant. "Are you sure? The punishment for desertion is death." He showed her where to make her mark, and she made it.

##

Realizing Stefan wasn't there and growing restless for the next phase of her mission.

She was hoping to leave for Denmark without violence, but her sergeant and two colleagues found her before departure. They provided her with a horse and several fine weapons for the trip. Not willingly, of course.

They say six months is incredibly fast to make the trip from Bendery to Jutland in those days. Of course, Charles himself supposedly made the trip in 15 days. For Cleo, six months it was.

The black death had hit Copenhagen, so the king wasn't there. "They are at Koldinghaus," said an innkeeper. You can see it in two weeks, if you can afford a costume. There will be a masquerade ball."

Cleo was intrigued, and found a silk dress and mask. She met a young confidant, the Countess Anne Sophie Reventflow. They were standing together when the king made his entrance.

"So skinny and pale," said Sophie. "Ah, but where a king may disappoint your eyes, he will please you in many other ways."

"Ha, he is married." Responded Sophie.

"Unhappily so, they say," said Cleo.

"I am too young for him," said Sophie.

"Flirt with your eyes. I believe you are perfect for him." Sophie appreciated the confidence. Her father had introduced the territories of St Thomas to the monarch, but everyone treated Sophie as if she was just a child.

When they were introduced, Cleo stared at the ground. Sophie, on the other hand, was animated. Before the end of the night, she and the king were dancing.

Sophie invited Cleo to visit the Reventflow estate. There were other suitors, but Cleo suggested they could not rival the king.

"He sent a messenger," Sophie said one day, with an air of excitement. "How do you plan to make love to a king?" Cleo asked her, then shared many ideas. Sophie had her chance... and the result was a rather ostentatious gift.

The palace at Vallo.

Cleo visited often. What else would she have to do, other than keep track of European armies in the field or court intrigue?

Then there was the visit from the King. Before his playtime with Sophie. Cleo took the opportunity to congratulate Frederick regarding his victory at Gadebush. "There aren't many kings who still lead troops in combat. His Highness is to be congratulated."

"It appears your cousin has risen from the dead," she added.

"Ah yes, Charles. It would be nice if he just stayed dead," stated his Highness grimly. "If his Majesty is sincere in this regard, your loyal subject has reliable men who can tend to the challenge."

"Sincere indeed," answered the king.

"Sophie, have them give my dog to the ship captain. He will recognize the assassin after the mission is complete."

"A dog?" asked the King. "Yes, it can be arranged," said Sophie.

Changing again to the garb of a man, Cleo found her flintlock and completed travel to the Danish front lines at Fredrickshald. With an introduction as a sharpshooter and proof via demonstration, the Danes were happy to allow her study of the Swedish and Danish earthworks. They told her about the skirmishes to date and where the famous king placed himself. She considered where he would place himself on the battlefield in the coming days. The next day, she was wrong: no Charles. Two days hence, however, there he was.

Cleo considered distance. She studied the sway of leaves and grasses in the wind. Then she waited for the king to pause, to correct or comment. She squeezed her trigger, with the inevitable delay of ignition that was a function of the technology of the day. She held the kick and explosion of her flintlock with resolute grip and gaze.

At the other end of her barrel, where the king had been, she saw a rider-less horse. She turned to the subaltern at her side and handed him the rifle. "That should make things a bit easier."

Before the young man quite understood what she was talking about, Cleo had extracted herself from the earthworks and soldiers. There was one sergeant who asked, "Where do you think you are going?" but at that moment she jumped on her waiting horse and was gone.

She found the ship in the port at Fredrickshald. Wolf recognized her. The captain gave the command to weigh anchor. Evidently Cleo had secured her berth on that ship for America.

Yet as they cleared port, Cleo noticed a look of concern on the Captain's face. He was gazing at a Dutch man of war… the Katwijk.

"Is there a problem?" Cleo wondered. "We will know in a minute," the captain answered. "Usually Danish vessels join British/Dutch convoys with no issue, but the Katwijk is behaving… strangely."

Cleo followed the captain's gaze, scratching Wolf behind the ears. She wandered back to her berth and found the sun-god dagger in her luggage. "I hope I won't need this," she thought to herself as she fastened it to a strap on her petticoat. "Sadites," she said to Wolf, and, as he sat, she tossed him a scrap from the day's breakfast.

##

New Holland in 1725. Financial markets. How does an assassin make a living in a colony? What was ISIS thinking? There was a fight between the gangs of New York. Who would sew these people back together after clubs, axes and long knives crushed bone and cut flesh?

"I will," thought Cleo. No one questioned the presence of a woman at the hospital. Credentials were less of an issue in the early years of the 18th century.

Wolf enjoyed fetching pieces of splint and discarded lacrosse balls. Through the years, Cleo noticed his bound grew shorter, his paws less quick. One day she wondered how long this creature would live, and thought a long hike might be nice.

On the other side of the Hudson, he sat at her side, gazing at the colors streaming through the skies. Cleo scratched him behind the ears and turned to gaze at his grey muzzle. Behind them, the rumble of a momma bear.

Cleo swatted the side of the bear's head, then gripped it by the throat. If bears had words, this one would have been thinking "What the Hell?" Cleo stared into its beady eyes and threw it fifty or so yards, watching it tumble while its cubs yowled after it. Cleo gathered Wolf into her arms and crawled into the cave. Her fingers stroked his soft head and ears as she drifted to sleep. In the distance, the bear had opted to find a new cave.

Taigen

Men (and women, in the modern age) have always prayed before battle. We seek any advantage, of course, and then there is always the prospect that we will meet our maker on the fields of the day, so best to do so with a reconciliation of sorts.

In early October, some 700 years after the birth of Christ, several knights went searching for the relics of a saint. Twenty years before, Tariq bin Zayid, a general of the Umayyad caliphate, had crossed the straits at Gibraltar into Europe, burning boats to convey the message, "We aren't going back," or more poignantly, "You boys better fight hard." In Arabic, of course.

General Zayid made an impression: his army fought fiercely. Even the English, protected by their channel, had heard "A plague of Saracens wrought wretched devastation and slaughter upon Gaul." After twenty years with so rarely a defeat, and outnumbering the Gauls more that 2:1 (80,000 to 30,000), Rahman, a new name under Allah's will, rode ferociously into battle.

But we were talking about the day before. The two armies had been staring across the fields selected by Martel, blocking the Moors advance to Tours, where Adb al Rahman was interested in looting the Basilica of St Martin.

Imagine their surprise. These knights had opened a box expecting to find the relics of a saint, when out jumped a soldier, dressed in linens and brandishing an antique sword. He won't hear the words "Taigen Sessai" for several hundred years, so everyone calls him, "man." That's it. Not "The Man," or even capitalized "Man." Just "man." Even though he isn't really a man. But more on that later.

They hastily brought the man, who understood not a word of the Frankish language, to Charles, who agreed this must be a miracle from the Lord (imagine how surprised they would have been to learn Sessai had met

Yeshua!!). They outfitted the man with 70 pounds of armor and replaced his sword with one of the rare Germanic (maybe… the source of these is still a mystery) broad swords.

Perhaps the Gauls would have held like a block of ice against the unarmored Saracens that day, with or without Sessai. Indeed, the exploits of that super-human swordsman, cutting horse and human alike, have been lost.

What isn't lost, however, is that Charles stopped the advance of the Muslim marauders that day. That new general, Rahman, fell, and his soldiers retreated, continuing to pillage as they went.

It was true that Sharia law existed even then, and living under it disadvantaged anyone who wasn't Muslim. For that, alone, the Christians might have fought against the Saracen invaders. Truth be told, however, Sharia would have been a reasonable burden. These Saracen soldiers acted like any other brutal invading force observed through time immemorial. The fight wasn't about Sharia. It was about a proud living for sons, honor and happiness for daughters.

##

If you were a crow and flew above camp for bread crumbs or other scraps, you would have seen a circle of massive wagons. Tied to these wagons, were horses of vast number. Inside these, Mongols, tents and fires. The aroma of smoke filled the air, just raw charcoal, perhaps burnt flesh, someone's dinner, or breakfast.

Donetsk has been a site of bloodshed multiple times in Ukraine history. As the Mongols advanced toward Europe, the renowned Mongol general, Subatai, requested permission from the Khan to attack Kievan Rus. While waiting for a reply, the Rus attacked, overly enthusiastic to witness the Mongol withdrawal.

Ultimately, the withdrawal served to be a Mongol ruse, extending opposing forces across a hundred miles. Sessai joined the battle formation when the Mongols halted their withdrawal. Anxious to press for what he thought would be a victory, one of the Rus leaders (there were several; unity of command was not something the Rus army achieved that day), Mstislav, attacked formed lines of Mongols at the Kalka river without waiting for the rest of his formation to catch up.

Beaten badly on the field, the Rus retreated to the safety of a fortified camp. they ultimately surrendered to the Mongols expecting release. Yansheng, Boye and Sessai were all standing observing when the Rus left camp. Subatai stayed long enough to watch the first lay down arms, a precedent that continued. But when they had put sufficient distance between themselves and weapons, given presumably to guarantee safe passage, someone gave the order to attack.

"But they have surrendered," said Boye, incredulous. "You heard the order," answered Yansheng, mounting and removing an arrow from his quiver. Sessai spurred his horse, and Boye followed close behind. It was a slaughter that day… only Mstislav the Bold and a few in his retinue were able to escape.

This wasn't the first massacre known to human kind. But it was ruthless enough to trouble a lifetime of sleep for some of the perpetrators.

##

Near the edge of camp, man was strapping a broadsword to a pack on a mule. He mounts his horse, pulling his mule, and nods to the sentry. The sentry nods back. "Enough," mutters man, as he rides his horse/mule train through a gap in the wagons to the road. He thinks about Kublai Khan's defeat of Kiev, no prisoners taken, and the defeat of Moscow. He thinks about a city the Great Khan was building near a city your century calls Beijing.

He thinks of Nanjing, the rustic town, where he plans to live, at least for a time. Of the books, he, man, contributed to a library built there. He thinks of the librarian and the farmers he knows, from the Horde, and pondered the quiet lives they must be living, as his horse wound around a hill, large enough to obscure the camp from view. Man can hear the horde. Smell them. But he cannot see them any longer. The hill is big enough and in the way.

The Hexi corridor in that day was safe and well-traveled. That said, the road was steep in Wushaolin, so he dismounted and walked. Man reflected on battles fought and his passion to acquire the best blade in the world. He remembered the sword he had seen, the razor sharp edge and tough, flexible response during a parry with his own broad sword. In comparison, lighter in weight, and thus an advantage, should he ever meet a superior warrior.

He also pondered where he might find such a sword, whether they would still be made in the location he had been provided, but more importantly, how he would manage to arrive there. The trip to Sandong was long indeed, but the trip across the Yellow Sea, and the Sea of Japan, would require a boat. Such passage was expensive. Man contemplated his pack and wondered how valuable an exceptional sword might be to a ship's captain. He would need treasure to acquire the katana, so hoped not to squander it on passage.

In the distance, thunder. Not the thunder of a charging horde, or even a casually marching one. But many hooves, none the less. Perhaps an opportunity for a fresh mule. Man increased the pace, to catch the herd, and shortly gazed into the blank face of a Kazak.

"Kazak in China?" man asked.

"Horses for Kublai." Replied the Kazak.

"Who can I talk to about a mule?" man asked.

"We haven't many mules, but you can ask Dankan." Kazak motioned with his chin to the front of the herd.

Man road to the front of the herd, asking for Dankan. Finally, he found a short fat man with a feathered cap. "My mule needs a rest," man said. "I have gold."

Dankan nodded. "Where are you headed?" he asked, eyeing man's broadsword.

"Shandong" man replied.

"We are going as far as Dunhuang. You are a freelance sword?" Dankan asked.

"Not really," replied man. "Recently released from the Horde. A traveler, returning home."

"You know the way?" asked Dankan, with a smile. "Roughly," said man.

"If we need you, you will draw your sword to help?" Man nodded. Dankan glanced around. If man was part of an ambush, denying his request would do no good anyhow. "You may travel with us. We can put your load on another mule tomorrow morning." he said.

"Very well," said man.

Man pulled back a bit and examined the herd. Smaller, perhaps, but in fine shape. Kublai will be pleased. The market in Dunhuang is an excellent place for stock to trade hands. Also, an excellent place to spend a few days. Man remembered the caves in Kiev and wondered how the caves here would compare.

Smaller caravans moving at a slower pace or coming from Dunhuang moved off to the side of the road. A silk caravan sat motionless. Man glanced at each of the riders, dismounted, holding steeds and watching the passersby. Man knew they were wary and assessed who served sword for such a small, but probably highly profitable group. More than one, no doubt. And at least one held in reserve, someone an observer wouldn't suspect. "I think I know," thought man.

Dust and thunder. Thunder and dust. The saddle chafed and man hardly noticed. So many years in a saddle. So many years in this saddle. But never this trail. The rock formations… the prickly trees, some plants, little yellow flowers. Slowly the sky filled with streaming colors, and Dankan called for camp.

"Is it true you fought with Subatai?" a boy asked. man glanced at Dankan, who pretended to be occupied elsewhere. "It is true," man responded. "I traveled from England, and heard rumors of the great Mongol general. Since I was searching for the best sword in the world, I thought I would find this general." The boy was attentive. Dankan was not.

"My trip to find him took two years, filled with many adventures, but the adventures once I joined Subatai's army were even greater." The boy smiled. "Tell. Tell!"

"I found Subatai's army just before the Battle of Kalka River. Early one morning I met a boy, not much older than you. Boye was his name. Boye and his family were from China and they were fascinated with my broadsword." Man produced his broadsword and revealed 12 inches.

Boy touched the broadsword, sharp but not biting. He gazed at man while putting the testing finger in his mouth. "Boye's father told me to follow them into battle. On that day, I didn't have a horse, but I was proficient with my broadsword. It was some years before I would meet Subatai, but this battle was quite a memorable one, and a famous one for him."

"Of course, during battle, if a man dies and drops from his horse, it isn't theft to take his animal. So very early, a Mongol arrow found a Rus knight, who met the Maker enjoying the bite of my broadsword. I jumped upon the rider less horse and rode after Boye. Boye's band almost sent arrows toward me, since the horse had Rus tack, but they saw the Mongol banner and recognized my armor. I rode between Boye and his father, as we swept in and out of the Rus ranks."

"You already knew how to ride a horse?" asked the boy.

"Well," said man, smiling, "I learned much more after joining the Horde."

"Enough," said Dankan. "We have many miles to go before we arrive at Dunhuang. Plenty of evening fires to enjoy with the fiction of the trail," he added with a sneer. Very well, thought man.

The Silk Trail was quite safe under the protection of Kublai Khan. Man's broadsword remained mostly in its sheath, except where a tale for boy required a showing.

##

There were other eras when the Silk Trail was more dangerous. The best evidence for this observation is the Great Wall, and one of its features, the Jade Gate. Designed to protect against numerous, marauding armies, the Wall has no equal in Europe, or indeed the known world, of man's day or even ours. The French Maginot Line, perhaps more awe inspiring for its firepower, if not for its longstanding reputation for being impenetrable.

Since this isn't a tale about the proper herding of horses, or the best rhythm for rest of its escorts, nor is it a travel tale for those intending a long trip within the borders of China, we won't belabor the details that emerged with man and his Kazak hosts. Man was happy to have found them, and they him, though there was no bloodshed this trip. Perhaps someone had heard of man's reputation.

Herding the merchandise through entrance to the Jade Gate was a bit of a challenge, since horses don't like small passages and a divided party is a vulnerable party. Dankan went through the passage first, with his best horse handlers and several of his swordsmen/archers. The remaining horse handlers brought up the rear, guiding all of the rearing, sprinting, kicking, biting livestock into the narrow passageway. Man went through with his mule somewhat after the last of Dankan's booty.

They continued along the trail, with the road growing more crowded the closer they came to Dunhuang. At night prior to entering the city, Dankan reminded his team of plans for the transfer of livestock, how he would settle salaries for each, and finalizing how much time was available for carousing before they would begin a return trip, for those who were returning to Kazakhstan.

Man said his farewells that night, gave a small Rus dagger to boy and thanked Dankan for his patronage. Dankan had a few ideas for finding companions, even work, for the trip to Xian, and man was grateful for this also. Dankan was grateful that boy had been entertained, even educated, and that this trip didn't require man's broadsword expertise.

It was a short trip from the camp outside Dunhuang to the Mogao caves. "Your health is excellent, bhikkhus?" asked man, his hands meeting in front of his chest, tipping his head.

Bhikkhus nodded, touching his own hands. "And yours?" he asked, in return.

"I am thankful," replied man. They both turned to reflect upon the giant Buddha, simultaneously kneeling, hands together at face level, bowing. They stood and walked on.

"Some time ago, I met a Man who proclaimed a supreme being, The Father. I am attempting to reconcile his teachings with those of our teacher."

"You aren't the first to raise these questions. Buddha would remind you that many lives have been lost or badly altered in the struggle regarding which theology is supreme to the others."

"Yes, but that isn't the reason Buddha rejected the idea of a supreme being."

They turned to a painting, of a lavish court scene, and Buddha's peaceful face. Again, they knelt, again they bowed. "No, that is true," said bhikkhus.

"Unfortunately, I haven't many days here, but I hope to supplement my understanding of the Buddha." Again, they turned to a painting, kneeling, bowing. "Why can't you stay?"

"I must go to Japan," said man. Bhikkhus nodded, studying man solemnly. "And why is that?" asked bhikkhus. Man turned to face the question. "I will purchase some weapons there."

"You are going there to kill?" said bhikkhus, without the air of judgement that man felt.

"I am not going to invade. I am interested in the quality of work from there," said man. "But you may kill when you are there?" Man studied the eyes of bhikkhus.

"In my time, I am frequently offered a choice, to live or die. I have chosen to live, and will do so again. This choice is usually forced on me, it isn't one I have taken for myself. The same is true, but even more so, for me in Japan. I wish to continue my studies of the Buddha, to clarify these teachings in my slow comprehension." Man touched his forehead with a finger.

"You go to Japan for a weapon. In any event, you might choose to stay here instead. So, it is a choice for you, even if you refuse to admit that it is." Man said nothing in reply. The two walked on. In front of a narrow door, bhikkhus stopped. "Wait here," he said. Man knelt and bowed. When bhikkhus returned, man lifted his eyes.

"Do you read Sanskrit?" asked bhikkhus. Man stood, answering "no."

Bhikkhus handed man five scrolls. "If it is true, that you wish to study, you will find teachers in Japan also. At a sacred place called Omine."

"You are too kind," said man.

"I sense the spirit of the Buddha with you. Your journey is an important one. Do not fail it." Man knelt, placing the scrolls aside, and bowed toward the bhikkhus. "Thank you for your generosity, thank you for your wisdom," man said. Bhikkhus bowed slightly and walked away.

Outside, man collected his horse and mule. He found a spare pouch and placed the scrolls in it, closing the pouch and wrapping it with a leather string. He mounted, considering his good fortune.

In the center of town, man found a group of pepper traders on the way to Xian. "You are satisfied with your protection," man asked the leader. "The road isn't very dangerous, under the Great Khan's protection," answered the leader.

"I spent years riding with the Horde. There may be benefits to having me along." The leader squinted, contemplating man's claim. "You can prove this?" he asked.

"You have heard of Subatai?" man asked, handing the leader a copy of man's release, with one of the more impressive signatures of the day. "I will pay you fourteen days' wages," said leader.

"We are traveling to Xian. I hear that is a eighteen-day trip," answered man.

"That's my offer," said leader. "Including the passage across the Yellow River at Lanzhou."

Man contemplated the offer. "When do we leave?" man asked. "Tomorrow," answered the leader. "I wish to sell you my mounts for the remaining four days," answered man. While leader inspected his horse and mule, man added, "and I will need your patience while I find a boat for a trip to Jinan."

"We will help you find such a boat. Very well," said leader. "I will take you to our camp."

At the outskirts of Dunhuang, pepper leader introduced man to his team of a dozen traders. Everyone was armed, but only several appeared formidable. Man deposited his pack with one of the capable men, then took his horse and mule to join the other mounts, a mix of camels and horses.

Pepper leader was up early that next morning, and the caravan was loaded, on the road, at sunrise.

The first and second days of the trip were monotonous, with little conversation. Halfway through the third day, five reputed members of the Horde confronted pepper leader, requesting a toll. Man rode to leader's side and began jovially comparing battle experiences with the five. After thirty minutes of banter, the five exchange glances and ride off. Leader nods. "Okay, that was worth eighteen days."

Two thirds of the trip came before Lanzhou and the wide Yellow River that ran through it. The mounts loaded on a flat bottom boat, while several of the men (including man) rode two sheepskin rafts across.

The road from Lanzhou to Xian was a busy one, and man found more former representatives with the experience of the Golden Horde, although no one else attempted to extract a toll from pepper leader. When at last they arrived in Xian, pepper leader escorted man to a busy river port and spoke with a trader about fare on his flat bottom boat, to Jinan.

"You will have to pay six days for a ticket," said pepper leader. "Can your trader friend send a message ahead, to my colleague in Jinan. Yansheng is the prefect there."

Pepper leader raised eyebrows and asked the question. In answer to the shaking head, he suggested, "Better to find your friend when you arrive." Man agreed. selling his mule and horses after loading packs on the boat, pepper leader embraced his new protector and took man's mule and horse.

River travel from Xian to Jinan was quieter than the Silk Road. Villages along the way, an occasional child running along with the boat, or water buffalo chewing river grasses. Finally they arrived.

Man thought the stink and bustle of Jinan was not nearly as bad as Xian. Finding Yansheng's office was easy, while reviewing safekeeping of pack from boat, purchase of a horse and mule with Yansheng's staff went smoothly.

##

"Ah, old friend," said Yansheng. Man bowed.

"Please, no bows between old war comrades. See how you haven't aged?"

"Ah, the troubles of battle and travel are nothing compared to the trials of prefecture governance," said man. Yansheng laughed. "To what do I owe your visit? Have you decided to try your hand at administration of an empire, after being so successful at winning it?"

"I want to spend some time with Boye and his family, then go to Japan," man said. "I have come into possession of some valuable Sanskrit texts from the Buddhist lord, which I hoped might secure passage to Japan."

Yansheng smiled at him. "There are no boats. The great Kublai is gathering all the boats. You might as well travel with the Horde."

"I don't want to attack Japan." Said man. "I just want to go there."

"I can't help you with that," said Yansheng. "although I can send a guide with you to Boye's farm. He is doing well. Rich farmland."

"Ah," said man, gathering his Sanskrit texts. "Tell me then, how I find Boye."

"First, we eat, then you rest. My staff will have your pack loaded and horses ready tomorrow, or latest in two days."

"You are too kind," said man.

##

Boye laughed. It was a good feast, and man was keeping his manners, avoiding ogling any of Boye's many daughters. "Too long, since we have shared the saddle. And certainly, you are in need of a woman?"

Man remember Kiev... Boye had left before Moscow. "I am not ready to settle yet," he said in reply.

"Ohh, still an ambitious man. I have seen your pack. Plenty for a nice farm and even for dowry for my most beautiful daughter." Boye's eyes twinkled as he pushed another cup of soju toward man.

"I can accept your soju, but not the generous offer to join your family. But it has been quite wonderful reliving our exploits, at the edges of the massacre."

Boye's smile faded. "Yes." He raised a cup. "To souls in heaven."

"To souls in heaven." They all toasted.

More pork, more borscht. Boye's twinkling eyes returned. "I am seeking a boat to Kyoto," man said.

"Ah," answered Boye, thoughtful. "You know Kublai is taking boats for a Japanese campaign."

"Yes," answered man. "I don't want to fight them. I just want to go there."

"A spy?" asked Boye.

"No. I have left the horde." Boye gazed at his old friend. "That is what you would say, in any event."

"Perhaps," said man. "But it is true."

Boye inhaled, gazing at his old friend. "You know, Kublai has a terrible temper. If he thought I were allowing any boats to slip my grasp, it might be bad for me and my family."

Man pondered Boye's big family, the many splendored feast. "Things have gone well for you," said man. "I hope to visit again, for an even better feast. And perhaps an even more beautiful bride."

Boye smiled. "I can trust my old friend. I am loading a Korean boat. It sails for Jejudo at the end of the week. Probably won't take you to Japan, but perhaps can take you across the Yellow Sea."

"Excellent," said man.

##

Man finds her beautiful dark eyes piercing. With a brief respite turn to her first mate, who brought man, the aspiring passenger, from a soju cup on that Shandong farm, to a chair on this Lady's chun, she frowns, and return her penetrating eyes to man. "What shall I call you," she asks.

"Jung-gug-in, Mistress." He answers.

"Euee. You may call me Chulgoiin.. or Kisaeng. Mistress is also fine."

"Thank you, Mistress."

She turns again to the first mate. "Leave us." she opens a drawer and removes several sheets of paper covered with characters. man cannot read them, so after a quick glance, he returns his gaze to her beautiful piercing eyes, then respectfully away. Rumors, (true information?) suggest she is the wife of the captain, and makes the decisions on the boat. Man wonders what happened to the husband.

"Everyone assumes Goose, my husband, is in the main cabin. You will serve me in the second cabin. Is that understood?"

"Yes Chulgoiin."

"Goose has swum. But it is best for everyone, most particularly you, if we honor his memory as if he is still living in the main cabin. Understood?"

"Yes Chulgoiin."

"What you ask is a substantial request. Just the fare to Chejudo might cost someone such as yourself a lifetime of favor. Yet you ask to be brought to Kyoto. We will have to stop for provisions in Chejudo and again in Matsui. I have trade goods for Chejudo, but there is no guarantee we will find goods for Japan."

"Yes Chulgoiin." she licks her lips, which man finds gorgeous, luscious. "You must read your Yochik. If there is even the smallest infraction, a hundred lashes. Does Jung-gug-in understand?"

"Yes Chulgoiin," says man.

##

She offered the pages, covered with characters. "What did I tell you about violating rules."

Man gazed at the pages, the characters appearing to be pretty birds of many varieties. "Mistress, these birds do not fly for me."

She gazed at him and gathered his meaning. "Such a poet, my Jung-gug-in. Step to the X."

Man obediently walked to an X in the room and held his hands to the arms jutting toward the ceiling. Mistress bound his hands with red leather straps. "Not strong enough, should I choose to resist," thought man. She removed his clothing. "Spread," she said, then she bound his ankles to the arms growing from the deck in their secret room.

"Whose fault is it that Jung-gug-in has a bad education?" Mistress asked, lashing him five times.

"Mine," responded man, wondering what she will do this time. Five more lashes. "And whose fault is it that you haven't spent enough time reading our rules," Mistress continued.

"Mine," answered man. The lashes helped him remember, in spite of it all, I am still alive.

Ten more lashes. "Yes I am," thought man. "Yes I am," he thought again as she touched him.

##

"There are pirates," she said. "Perhaps you allow me on deck," man said to his Mistress. She considered his request. "It is true, you are no use to me if I lose this boat."

"Yes, you have nothing to lose at this stage," man said, smiling.

She didn't smile. "Very well."

Man stepped to his chest and pulled it from the wall. He reached behind, finding his broad sword. He unsheathed twelve inches, which sparkled as his own eyes were sparkling. Still no expression on the beautiful face of Mistress.

Man went to the door, opening it, and strode onto the deck. He quickly saw First Mate. Man tipped his head to First Mate. "What?" asked Mate, clearly busy with preparations. Man knelt, gazing up at Mate. "Keep your warriors in reserve. I will take the first wave with this," again, unsheathing twelve inches of sparkling steel, and resheathing them. "Take the second wave with your archers." The First Mate nodded grimly. "Then I will lead a boarding party of ten," said man.

As the hooks of the boarding net took hold, Jung-gug-in knelt at the farthest bow-side hook. As the first pirate became visible, man ran the length of the gunwale, his broad sword finding more than one jugular. Only one of the pirates' arrows found Jung-gug-in, his forearm, where upon man knelt, coaxed the arrow a bit further through his arm, then broke off the barbed tip. As man removed the arrow, the First Mate's archers took the next wave… and the few pirates from the first wave who hadn't met man's broadsword.

Mate's archers moved to the gunwale and began targeting archers on the ship's deck (those in the rigging had already fallen). Mate and his nine skirmishers followed Jung-gug-in over the side, onto the pirate vessel.

After moving pillage to Mistress's chun, Mate took control of the pirate vessel with two of his skirmishers. Jung-gug-in and Mistress agreed it would make an excellent gift to Kublai.

They bid First Mate an "anyi goshipsheyo," then second mate assessed a new course for Jejudo. Man returned to his room. Mistress smiled.

##

He had many visits to the deck, and enjoyed the beauty of the Yellow Sea. Sun rises, sun sets, swells and rolling seas. Boats that passed in the distance. Glances from the crew. No one asked any questions, no one even spoke.

With a glance from Mistress, man always promptly returned to his room.

##

After docking at Jejudo, Man wasn't allowed from the room.

Music started. She came in, a beautiful dress. "Today, you are master," she said. Her face was as radiant a beauty as man had ever seen. And never, in two thousand years, had man enjoyed the bliss felt that day.

Her dress was an orange silk with purple dragons twisting up, down and around. Dragon ropes fastened the overlapping cloth, draping and wrapping the Mistress curves. She swayed with the ten tone notes, obscuring the harmony in her face with a fan. Man caught her arm and kissed her on the lips.

Mistress stopped her dance. She frowned at man, then after a wide backswing, slapped him as hard as he had ever felt her swing. "I thought I was master," said man. "Have respect. This gift I have for you, do not interrupt." Man blushed. Mistress shuffled away. After the refrain, she slowly began the motions of the dance again. It would be some time before her lithe frame, somehow unrestricted by the narrow pencil of the silk dragon dress, resumed its fluid motion.

Her motion, contains the elegance of a swan… the fan, her own plumage. Slowly his embarrassment faded, as he considered how his own efforts to move so, had he set out to try, might have ultimately appeared in such a costume, with such movements. She swam around him, her eyes hiding, then flitting across the sights that are man, then flirting with his eyes.

She lured him in, slowly. He thought of her promise, that he is master today, and wondered, what truly does that mean? He considered the freedom to view, to touch, the subtle strength of her form, the soft velvet of her skin, considered all this as she continued her dance, spinning, first far away, then closer, closer, and finally spinning around within inches of his limbs, face, fingers…

Until finally, she stopped, in a rigid bow. Six inches from his face, her dark brown eyes sparkled, seeing in man's face that her dance had its effect. She whispered, "you may kiss me now."

Catching the hem of the dress… he bowed to her art, her beauty, her form, and gently kissed the arch of her perfumed foot. Cautiously, he glanced up at her eyes, sparkling above the fan. "Okay?" He asked. She nodded.

With a respectful two hands, he lifted the hem of the orange dress, leaning carefully forward, his lips tenderly finding her ankle. "Okay?" He asked. Two strokes of the fan below her sparkling eyes was her answer. His lips brushed her calf, so strong, so warm after such a dance.

In answer to his glance, she smacked his head with the fan, a fan folded in the swing downward to his adventurous skull. "Yes," was her affirmation. Lifting her dress higher, much as a child might peek under the curtain his parents draped across his pile of birthday gifts, he exposed her right knee for a kiss, then her left one. It was her turn to blush when his lips found each thigh, but when the tip of his tongue found lace still higher, she once again slapped him across the face, this time harder than the other time.

He stood. "I am master now," he said, picking her up, easily containing her swinging punches and jabbing kicks. He bound one arm, then the other, holding her motionless as he carefully unfastened the green dragon cords. "You are fortunate I don't just rip this silk, these twines from your fortunate succulent form."

"Fortunate," she answered with a sneer… he released a hand and she slapped him with it. He bound that hand, then both ankles. Then slowly he took her for the first time. She struggled, but there was no stopping his fluid swoop, which soon found a rhythm in close answer to her own. Her cries, he knew, were no longer a protest.

Unfastening the lashes, he threw her to the bed. She welcomed a third kiss and wrapped her strong thighs around his waist.

##

At some point, the music had stopped. The motion of the ship transformed from a gentle back and forth of an at-port rocking… to the up and down swing of the open seas. When at last they opened the door to the deck, there were pitch dark skies and lanterns on the rigging.

"Wait," she said, scurrying to the main cabin. She opened the door and invited him in. Later, he fell asleep. When he awoke, she was gone. Man found his way back to the second cabin and fell asleep again.

##

The Tsushima Strait wasn't called that in those days. Island hopping was the safest way to move from the Korean Jejudo Island to Japan proper

"I will see you in heaven," she had said.

"But I won't be there," man had said… tears shamelessly streaming down. Man had never been so attached to a woman, and wondered how she always occupied his thoughts. Those long days and nights on the Yellow Sea, in the port of Jejudo, then crossing to

Japan. Her stoic goodbye. His response, "I have come for two blades, perhaps three. But I wish to stay with you."

Mistress was practical in her answer. "Your valor held wagging tongues for a time. But wag they will, in time. Neither you nor I have legal foundation. Only Goose, and my son."

"You have a son?" man asked, surprised. "We will talk about it more. In heaven," she said, smiling. That smile, so rarely had he seen anything so beautiful on this earth.

Man smirked. "I won't be there, Mistress," he reminded her.

"I think you will be," she replied. "Go," she commanded, and he hopped down the net to the skiff.

Vivid memories will keep me, thought man.

##

Man listened to First Mate and the Japanese trader. They glanced at him.

"You know something of Kublai Khan?" asked the trader.

"Something, yes," answered man.

"We understand he is gathering ships. For a trip to Japan?" asked the trader.

"The Great Khan is an ambitious man, but not a sailor," answered man.

"Why do you wish to go to Gifa?" asked the trader.

"I am interested in purchasing a sword," answered man. Man unsheathed 12 inches of the broad sword. "My steel is fine, but I understand the swords made in Gifa are the best in the world."

"Only samurai are permitted to own such swords," answered the trader. He returned to the conversation with First Mate.

After a time, First Mate stepped close. "I have arranged for an introduction to a local samurai, but you will only be able to keep a small pack and your sword. Wait until we have traded for provisions, then the trader will take you to the samurai."

Man nodded. He glanced at chun, at the robed Mistress at the gunwale. "Such sacrifices I make," he thought.

##

A lead samurai dismounted. Nose to nose, he asked man, although it was more a statement. "Your Kublai has set sail for Japan."

Man answered, "The Great Khan is an ambitious man, but not a sailor."

The samurai examined man's broadsword. "This is not permitted in Japan."

"It is a small grant that I was allowed," answered man. He hoped there wouldn't be violence here. The samurai smiled, perhaps a bit overconfident, thought man.

"I will also permit it," answered the samurai. "But we won't be going to Gifa. I need your services here in Osaka."

##

"There is a boat in the harbor." man turned to his samurai master. "We haven't had many visitors this year," said man. "Yes, the captain says he brought a passenger here, more than ten years ago." man raised his eyebrows. The samurai continued, "they do not have a name, only that they left a passenger."

man answered, "I may see the captain?" The Samurai nodded.

##

"You are my father," the captain said. He handed man an urn. "This is my mother. She wanted to be with you." man accepted the urn with somber face, somber thoughts. "You have traveled quite a distance to give me this. Can you stay a few days, perhaps a week?" man's son nodded, "Neh."

They exchanged more pleasantries. Even from the few platitudes, man realized the mate, and Mistress, had trained son well. When a few members of son's crew arrived on a skiff, man asked, almost pleading for the opposite: "You must go?"

"I must go," son's simple answer. "Certainly, my loss," said man, with a polite bow. man contemplating being on that ship again. Contemplated getting to know his son. But son bowed respectfully, then hopped on the skiff. He held a hand in the air, a confident, warm smile on his lips. man held his hand in the air in response. When the skiff made chun, son hopped up the net and onto his boat.

man stood watching the ship tack toward the horizon. The sky filled with colors, as the sun set, and the ship disappeared in the distance.

"Is everything alright, sensei?" The old samurai asked. man glanced at him, thinking about the katana that he still hadn't obtained, for which man sacrificed so much, while man's eyes found shadows arrayed across the dock, among crates and barrels. What answer can he give? man held the urn in both hands and thought of things that might have been. "Shall I dump her ashes in the bay?" man wondered. "No. I shall keep her, for a bit," he thought.

Man remembered kneeling at the foot of the cross. When that foolish soldier thrust the spear in His side, those eyes told man, "no." Then, before the famous last words, those eyes again locked with man's. "You will be there," He said. Suddenly, at last, man remembered those words, and understood what He meant. They say a vampire lost his soul upon the biting. Surely, man was deeply saddened to have found a soulmate, only to lose her to circumstance. The promise of an afterlife was a curious one to an immortal, but in this case, an encouraging promise.

Turning again to the horizon, man's eyes saw the black sea against night sky. He knew the sun would rise in the morning.

But the ship would still be gone.

##

The years went by, the years went passed slowly. Each year, on the anniversary of son's visit, man contemplated a ceremony for Mistress' ashes. Each year, man couldn't part with them, under a ceremony or any circumstance.

Summer passed to Fall passed to Winter passed to Spring passed to Summer again. Each Spring, the cherry blossoms bloomed. The fragrant flowers were always gone before summer. Man walked in the gardens. He learned Japanese, Chinese and how to read Sanskrit. He helped maintain the samurai's household.

The end of one winter, the samurai walked with him. "We will not stay much longer together, I am afraid," said the samurai. "Are you ready to resume your journey?"

"Yes, I am," said man.

There were few samurai who left this earth thru natural causes in those troubled times —most died from an assassin, in battle, or a hari-kari knife. Man's benefactor was one of the few. There was much conversation regarding who would do what, who would get what, among the samurai's family. No one remembered the threat of Kublai Khan, or even that man knew anything about the Chinese fighting force.

After a short conversation with samurai's heir, man liberated a small portion of what was left of his pack, and used it to buy a mule. He loaded the mule and bid the household goodbye.

After three days on the trail, the cherry blossoms emerged. Man smiled. The road became steeper and at last he arrived at Omine. The monks there were happy to have him, and man was able to find a small cave, behind a locked door, with a civilized room.

Man found the ticking lock he had made so many years ago, and affixed it to a new box. He climbed in and pulled the lid shut.

##

The lid popped. Light came in through the window. Man sat up. He gazed at his small room and hopped from his box. He inspected the treasure in a box and the long broadsword. He took the urn with her ashes from the mantle.

Holding the urn with both hands, he thought "the urn of memories." He placed it back on the mantle, selected several articles of appropriate clothing, then rolled the fine cloth around one of the Sanskrit scrolls. On his way out the door, man grasped a walking stick in the corner, then he locked the door as he exited.

"The rest can stay here," he thought. "It is time to go to Kyoto."

##

"The Lord will see you now," said the samurai. Man dropped to his knees, and crawled through the door. Truly, it wasn't much different in Japan from his experience at the court of the Great Khan.

Passing as a wandering samurai wasn't hard, and man was able to pass any sword test. Learned men were fascinated with his Sanskrit scroll. Man learned to play chess in the court of shogun and improved his understanding of Japanese characters, with comparisons to the Chinese.

After some months, man was approached by an Imagawa messenger. "There is a boy who needs a tutor. The shogun feels you might make yourself useful." The messenger bowed politely. "When do we leave?" asked man.

##

"It appears you have some practical, and some not so practical knowledge," said the Lord.

"Thank you, Lord." Responded man.

"You will tutor my son," instructed the Lord.

"Yes, my Lord." He turned to a toddler, moving toy boats across the floor.

"Taigen, say hello to Jung-gug-in." The toddler glanced at his father, then to his new tutor. "Is he smarter than the last one?" asked the boy.

"I think so," said the Lord.

Man observed Taigen Sessai move the boats waves opposing a "t." Man moved one of the boats. "Ah, Sensei pays attention," said the boy. Man smiled.

Every day they played with boats. Most days they played with soldiers. Some days they read Sanskrit texts. "You must not permit emotion," said man. "Emotion causes pain."

The boy glanced at his sensei. "Are you a monk?" he asked. "Yes, once I was," said man.

"Mount Omine?" asked the boy. "My papa wants me to live at Mount Omine someday."

Man contemplated this comment. "Perhaps you and I will move to Omine someday, but first we must learn something about these," said man, walking to a box. Inside were two wooden swords.

"Ah," said the boy, grasping both, then in a fluid motion, performed the first form.

"There are things you will teach me," said man, "but there are also things I will teach you."

The boy smiled proudly.

##

Man inspected the array of toy boats. "There are more this time," he said. "Yes," said the boy. "And why not? More boats are harder to beat."

"Harder perhaps, but not impossible," said man.

That evening, the boy's father expressed some concern. "There aren't many thieving bands or errant samurai on the road to Gifa, but occasionally one finds them."

"You have seen my blade work. With a borrowed blade and a few archers, I can protect him," responded man.

Taigen's father responded, "I will also send my best blade, Taigen's instructor. His maid and four samurai."

"Very well," answered man.

They left later that month. At the fire on the second night of the trip, instructor showed his blade to man. "Made by Kanesada," it said. Instructor showed man the haman, almost a stain on the blade, otherwise so smooth and polished, and the unoi, a sparkling line in the firelight, along the edge of the haman.

"We find Izuminokami Kanesada in Gifa. He is the best."

Man only nodded. Instructor opened a box. Inside, four lumps each of hagane, kawagane and shigane metals. "Two for you, two for Taigen." Man nodded again. "Thank you."

Finding Kanesada once they arrived in Gifa was not a challenge, although hearing truthful words proved to be. The party provisioned several rooms with a hospitable family. Kanesada promised the swords would only take several months.

Nearly every day, after studies and exercises, man, Taigen and instructor would watch Kanesada making those four swords. They watched him pounding the blades. Wrapping them in clay of varying thickness. And finally, testing the blades. How was it none of them broke? Finally, they watched him stamp the characters "Kanesada saku" and wrap the hilts around the tangs, where the stamps were made.

Halfway through the final process, a messenger arrived from Papa. "The time has come to go to Omine."

Taigen Sessai frowned. He glanced at man. "This means trouble," said Taigen.

##

Man enjoyed another trip on horseback, the Buddhist sayings, or conversations about tactics amid the mountains, valleys and fields of Japan. They talked about foot samurai, mounted samurai, about archers and about a new weapon, the arquebusier. As they got closer to Mount Omine, they spoke more and more about the duties and days of a monk. When they arrived, both boy and teacher were prepared. Instructor continued on the road, returning to the boy's father. Taigen was close to a master with his two katana.

Man was delighted to learn the door for his key was still there among the many in Omine, and his treasures (in particular the urn of memories and the broadsword) had not been disturbed in the years of his absence. Man told Taigen about the beautiful ship captain, in flowery words, and told the boy, becoming a man, about the wars in Europe and Asia. The broadsword was convincing evidence.

Together they pored over the Sanskrit texts and debated the tenets of Buddhism, and also whether there might be a Father. "It isn't a matter of what is best," said man. "What matters… is what is true." It was hard to explain to Taigen why man was so certain Yeshua was who He said He was, and that there indeed is a Father.

Together they made velvet cases for the katana. Man's case would hold two katana and his broadsword.

##

Dragging three dead assassins to the wounded boy, he released them and knelt crying. Man gazed into the dying face of a fine young man. "Too soon, to depart," he whispered. "Imagawa Yoshimoto will need you," said the boy. Man nodded grimly. "I won't let you down again," he replied.

"Who were they?" the boy asked. "Perhaps messengers from the Shinano lords. Or Akeche Mitsuhide," answered man.

Man stood after the last breath from his liege. He walked to the shiny looking glass. "Taigen Sessai," he said firmly, "you have much to do these next years."

In the court of Imagawa Yoshimoto, he was welcomed as the lord's uncle. "I expected a younger man," said Yoshimoto. "The weight of impending responsibility ages a man," responded the person responding to a new name. Taigen Sessai, much more fitting, though man had yet to earn the name.

##

Shouldn't we know the details of such battles? Three thousand warriors spread across the features of

Azukizaka, a second battle there. Most, foot samurai, but some nine hundred mounted, some eight hundred archers (with bows improved with Mongol composite construction) and almost three hundred arquebusiers. Or was it thirty thousand total?

Carefully infiltrating the woods, mountains and ravines of Okazaki, man had been able to position his soldiers where they might best surprise the Oda. man placed his soldiers where the waters of the Sugo and Iga rivers protected from surprise attack, while channeling opponents where Sessai might best trap and disarm them.

At this place, man earned his name, and Taigen Sessai earned his place in history. Retaking the castle at Anjo, perhaps not trivial, but to follow the Second Battle of Azukizaka, was an easier struggle.

Somehow the Oda were weakened, and Imagawa accrued what everyone thought was insurmountable army.

"I weary of battle," Taigen told his advisor. "Yoshimoto will be fine without you. But what shall I tell him?"

"Tell him I am dead," suggested Sessai. Taigen's advisor glanced in Taigen's eyes, a laugh on his lips. "You go to Omine?" the advisor asked. With a serious expression, man handed his advisor an urn. An urn engraved, "Taigen Sessai."

"Gout is a terrible thing," said Taigen. "Truly," said his advisor. They embrace. "Wait," said the advisor. He handed Sessai a short blade. "Thank you truly," said Sessai. Two Katana and a short sword.

The advisor wonders, one day, where the ashes in the urn came from. Messengers sent to Mount Omine cannot seem to find Taigen Sessai.

##

Returning to Mount Omine, Taigen Sessai avoided attention. He found a room he had prepared some years before. "A good place for a sleeping," thought Taigen Sessai.

The big box on a table. The table had shelves. The small room had a small fireplace, and a mantle.

Sessai placed the sword case, with swords, on the shelves under his big box. Glanced at the urn of memories on the mantle.

Sessai checked the door, locked and secure. Then he swung into the box, thinking "It is time," as he pulled shut the lid. Taigen fingered the short sword on his belly and drifted into another sleeping…

##

The box opens. Taigen's eyes open. Things are quiet.

"Well?" a voice asks. Taigen sits up and glances at a man he hadn't seen in a long, long time.

"Do you remember me?" the man asks.

"I do," answers Taigen Sessai.

"You have failed." Taigen takes a deep breath, the first in many, many years. "How this time?" he asks the man.

"Cleo is awake."

Taigen gazes at his feet. Hopping from the box, he attaches the short sword to his waist and gathers the velvet sword case on the shelf under the box.

"How?" Taigen asks. The man responds, "Two men broke into her crypt. They are both dead."

The man is morose. "Of course," Taigen answers. "Of course," affirms the man.

"I have commissioned a fast boat. It is in the harbor, flying a gold cross against a blue-sky banner. The Ukraine. There is a skiff at the pier with the first mate. He will take you to her. The crew believe you are a petty nobleman in the Russian court, considering allegiance to Ivan Mazeppa." Sessai stares at the man blankly. "They will fill in the details."

"Okay," answers Sessai.

"Have you ever met a vampire who woke from a thousand-year sleeping?" Sessai contemplates an answer.

The man continues. "Don't try to take her. Just contain the damage."

"Are you coming along also?" Asks Sessai. "No," is the answer. "There are two horses in the courtyard for you. Ride one until it can go no further, then leave it for the second." Then the man asks "Do you remember how to get to the port?" Reasonable question after a two hundred year sleeping.

Taigen nods. The man turns to leave, then says over his shoulder, "This Japan stay has been a financial success for you. Enough possessions are loaded in the boat to keep you for a few hundred years, and perhaps to provision an army. Just go to the boat. We can afford no delays."

Always so full of business, thinks Taigen Sessai. "Ok," he answers.

The man walks out, and Taigen walks to the urn on the mantle. He takes it down, holding it in two hands. "Perhaps I will keep her with me for a few more days," he thinks. Then then he walks to the horses, toward his fast ship of the East India Company.

##

"Permission to board," was greeted with a hand motion. The captain bowed slightly. "Here is your letter of introduction to Ivan Mazeppa," he said, handing over a scroll. If he thought there was anything out of the ordinary about his new passenger, the Captain wasn't admitting that. Sessai opened the letter and read.

The captain continued, "We will take you to Odessa. There is a guide there to take you the rest of the way to Kiev." Sessai turned to face the sea while the captain gave orders to weigh anchor.

Although he had seen much of the world, Taigen Sessai had not spent much time in boats, on the ocean.

He enjoyed the placid seas, and even the swells and valleys when the weather grew foreboding.

"Contain the damage," said the man, who woke him from his sleeping. Sessai wondered how that man had found his crypt. He wondered about the global breadth of the vampire order, who were complicit, and when he would be permitted to understand more of its function and make-up.

"Perhaps after I've managed to string a success or two together," thought Sessai.

The East India Company crew handed him to a guide in Odessa. The guide took him to see the bodies in Kiev, then to Ivan Mazeppa, the Hetman of Ukraine.

Sessai met a Cossack warrior, Stefan, there who had been recently ravaged. He fought alongside this Stefan at Poltava, but there were few survivors of that battle. So far as Sessai knew, Stefan was the only vampie/vampire Cleo had created, although Sessai had no idea how many had suffered the consequences of the two grave robbers. They hadn't seen her on the field at Poltava.

After his first sighting of her, Sessai rode Bendery, and spoke with Mazeppa. Presumably Cleo was attempting to find Stefan Cossack, for reasons known to the order. Sessai wondered what Cleo would do when frustrated.

Perhaps she would travel elsewhere in Europe. Asia. Perhaps even America. Sessai rode to Amsterdam next.

"I am attempting to find a murderer and deserter." Sessai's Dutch colleagues connected him with a ship of the line, the Katwijk. They would check ships heading to the new world for a female fugitive of dark complexion.

Sessai had no idea he had seen Isis on his trip to Amsterdam. He had no idea how close the Katwijk came to intercepting Cleo's travel. But in spite his diligence, and occasional small victory, Cleo slipped his grasp.

##

Much of Stefan's first two hundred year sleeping, Sessai spent in Ukraine, Western Russia and Poland, searching for Cleo. There was no sign of her. There were no tales of new vampies, no superhuman killings, for ten years. Then twenty. A hundred.

Sessai knew that Stefan would wake in 1910 or so. While he considered that Cleo might return to Ukraine, the samurai thought it more likely she would assume he was wandering. Thus, Stefan was left to his own devices upon awakening and managed to marry a kulak's daughter all on his own. Sessai observed from a distance.

When the Communists came from Russia, and seized Stefan's farm, Sessai followed him to Warsaw. Watched the father and daughter find a synagogue sleeping place there, then left to observe Bismarck Germany when he was certain father and daughter were safe.

STEFAN

It was a loud celebration, marking a historic time for Hetman Ivan Mazeppa. For the first time since anyone could remember (perhaps since the days of Kievan Rus?) the east- and west-bank Cossacks had been unified.

"Who is marrying whom?" Ivan Mazeppa shouted after the vodka was well enjoyed. Two of his warriors called out. Turning to his favorite warrior, Ivan called "Stefan, what about you? No woman for you?" Stefan hated being outdone. He thought of the beauty he noticed earlier, a tall brunette. She was hanging around the edges. No one knew who she was. When he grabbed her waist, she had softly whispered, "So you are the champion of the East Bank?"

Stefan saw her thru the smoke. "You there, come let us marry!" Cleo was there for information, resolute to avoid attention. She attempted to slip away, but someone grabbed her, lifted her above their heads, and passed her to Stefan, the champion of East Bank.

"Certainly you have no better man to take your hand." Cleo gazed at him and contemplated her options, choosing to play along. She walked quietly at his side, and, later, even into the champion's bed chamber later that evening. But the next morning, the champion was alone.

Several days later, another stranger appeared. Sessai asked about wounds to the Champion's neck, then, some days later thought he might join Mazeppa's cavalry. Though there were many better horsemen, there were none better with a sword.

##

From a downwind hill, they watched her kneel at the fork, studying the hoofprints. First one glanced through the telescope, then the other. She stood, pulling her hood from her head and lifting her nose into the wind. She glanced at a red dog, hardly a spot to her observers on a hilltop.

"Yes, that is her," said Stefan. "So that is Cleo," asked Sessai, grimly. "You are sure?" When Stefan nodded, Sessai continued, "She will assume we go with Mazeppa and follow him. You will be safe here. Unsure about her companion. Might be a werewolf."

Stefan glanced at him, touching the small scars on his neck. "Do you believe me now?" asked Sessai.

"Do I have a choice?" Stefan asked. They stood and walked into a small cave. Sessai gave Stefan the powder and pulled the cloak tightly. "You won't remember this for a long time, but you will know how to return to Mazeppa's lands. They will welcome you as a returned hero when they see the sword." There was a mark on the sword…

Stefan studied the sand timer/lock contraption in the box, then carefully climbed in, next to the sword.

"Sweet dreams," said Sessai, as he shut and locked the box.

##

There was a loud clicking sound, and the box lid swung open. Stefan opened his eyes… pitch black… he grasped a sword at his side, which helped him hoist himself from the box. Within minutes he found a wall that moved.

Stefan walked into the sunlight and took in the warm air, the singing birds… unable to remember why he was there and assessed the size of the rock that he had just displaced. He saw a road in the distance and walked to it. After getting there, he followed some wagon tracks east.

He arrived at a town mid-day and asked for a blacksmith, looking for work. The blacksmith took one look at the steel, Mazeppa's sword, dragged Stefan to a nearby inn.

The blacksmith pushed Stefan in front of the Kulak, and said "Gospodin, we have a visitor."

The man glanced at Stefan and shrugged. "So?" He asked, almost laughing. The blacksmith handed him Mazeppa's sword, at which point Gospozha stopped laughing. "Where did you get this?" he asked.

"My family," said Stefan. "Where are you from, man?" The kulak asked. "The West," was Stefan's brief reply.

"The West," repeated the farmer, who glanced at the blacksmith. "You need a job?" Gozpozha asked. "Yes, Gospodin," was the answer. "And some food." The Kulak pushed his plate to Stefan, then invited the newcomer to join the Kulak's team at the farm. "We need help," he said, simply but also took possession of the sword, promising Stefan that he would watch it until Stefan chose to leave, should that day come.

Stefan glanced at the farmer, then at the blacksmith, then listened to Gospozha: "Work on the farm is hard, but it's the best place on the East Bank. I need a foreman. If you have come by this sword honestly, I will be able to tell quickly."

A two hundred year sleeping makes a man hungry. Very hungry. Stefan inhaled the food on the plates in front of him. Then the farmer took him to the homestead, a place that would be his home for the next fifteen years.

A few days later there was a dance, kind of a folk gathering. Stefan's first, but a monthly occurrence in those days, certainly the high point of the month for everyone in the village. Couples and Cossack dances. Stefan joined in, and proved quite good at that distinctive Cossack dance. His new friends christened him "Cossack"… Stefan Cossack. And it impressed the Kulak's daughter, that dance.

Stefan saw her, watching him dance, laughing with the other girls. She was radiant, a beauty. Someone whispered that she was Gozpozha's daughter.

##

There were crowds the night before. Shouts in the street. Words about the downfall of the Tsar. Glorious words about a new Rada Verkovna. The people's power.

Stefan found the blade, the one that caught Gozpozha's eye. He held it in the air. In truth the shouts were intoxicating. So many torches. But then, suddenly, the screaming. In the distance.

Stefan was with her mother. A happy night. But he burst into the living room, when the screams began. She could hear him from upstairs. Then outside, and onto a horse. Even the new kulak didn't have a car then.

When Stefan returned, there were more voices. Two little girls, a little boy. A man. A woman.

The next morning, Stefan had gathered them all around the hearth and swore them to secrecy. Introduced his family to this new family. "My wife, Evalyn," Stefan started. "My eldest son Pavlo, eight. Olya, six. And our youngest boy Stevan, three." The

Jewish father, Adam, introduced his family next. After giving them new names, Stefan announced, "It's time to get to work."

"May I come along, Papa," Olya asked that day. Perhaps he didn't want to cause alarm or show fear of the roving mobs. Stefan said, "Yes."

Olya remembered the summer breeze caught her hair that morning, and brushed it across her cheek. It wasn't the first time she had jumped, but it was the highest. She was walking through the grasses and saw, under the tree, that a little bird had fallen from its nest.

Papa was working in the field with the new family. She gently picked up the bird, then glanced at Stefan. Shall I ask for his help, she had wondered. Looking up, she saw a bird's nest 75 feet up the tree. The branches were plenty apart until there. Taking one last glance at Papa, she jumped.

Catching a branch next to the nest, resting a foot on the lower branch, Vanessa gently placed the bird with its brothers and sisters.

"What are you doing," Stefan asked sternly. Vanessa glanced down at him. How did he get there so fast? she wondered. "Rescuing a bird, Papa," she had replied. His gaze turned from her to the fields where he was working. "Get down here right now," he had said. Obediently, Vanessa climbed from the tree.

Stefan gazed at his daughter. He had always thought she was a remarkable girl… what father does not think this of his child? But what he had witnessed could only mean one thing, and Stefan wasn't sure how it was possible or what to do about it.

Sessai had been quite clear. He effectively shared how monstrous Cleo's biting had been, and shared some of the horrific events she had been party to creating in human history. Stefan had gone into his sleeping convinced that pacifism was an excellent choice and that, if carefully lived, his life albeit a long one, might resemble that of a normal human being.

Sessai had adopted abstinence, but hadn't required a celibacy oath from Stefan. Nor had there been any suggestion that, if Stefan had children, that they might inherit his curse. Or was it a blessing?

His daughter had jumped the rest of the way down and was standing in front of him. "Oh princess," he told her, kneeling so his head was level with her's: "you must never do that again."

"But Papa, you don't like birds?" She had asked innocently.

"Dearest," he said smiling quietly, "of course I like birds. But that jump!" He glanced at her, "have you ever jumped that high before?"

"Well, I am a good jumper, Papa, but this was the highest yet." Vanessa was proud.

"Have you ever seen anyone else jump so high?" her father asked her. "Have you seen your brothers do so, or anyone else." Vanessa had paused, looking thoughtful. "umm. No Papa."

"Have you had jumping contests with your brothers?" Stefan asked. Suddenly he was concerned that all his children might have inherited the order. "Well," Vanessa had replied earnestly, "Pavlo is a very good jumper but not nearly as good as me." Making note to check his son for normalcy, Stefan grasped both Vanessa's wrists.

"Princess, this is very surprising to me. I also am like you." Stefan continued, "But I have only met two other people who can jump so high, and I haven't seen them for many, many years."

He looked intendedly into her eyes. "Olya, this is a monstrous strength! You must never do it again!" Vanessa's eyes began to tear: "Papa.. Papa… am I a monster?" she asked earnestly.

Stefan took a deep, deep breath. "Oh princess," he responded, taking her into his arms, hugging her firmly. He backed away again, looking into her eyes. "Do you think I am a monster?" he asked his daughter.

"Oh no, Papa, you are an angel!" she had reflexively responded. Stefan smiled, laughing gently. "Yes, yes. You and I, Olya, we can decide to be an angel.. or a monster. Which do you want to be?" He asked.

Vanessa nodded her head, "Oh, I am an angel, I want to be an angel." Stefan smiled, hoping he had found a way to communicate what he must. "Yes, Olya, I want you to be an angel too. But you must never hurt anyone or even show anyone, how strong you are, and how high you can jump. Do you understand?"

Vanessa appeared thoughtful. "Well, I guess I understand. But… why can't I just be myself?"

##

In truth, Stefan had many more issues to be concerned with as Olya grew into her own. His new father-in-law had become one of the most successful farmers in the region, but times were not good for financial success. The earth of farms near Zhytomyr was black, as rich as they came in Ukraine. Grains grew in abundance, filling wagons full, and in turn barges, to Kiev and even down to ships that traveled the Mediterranean.

But the heritage of Mazeppa's sword wasn't enough to unify a people so long under the thumb of an Empire. It takes time to learn about one another, and about what is right. Stefan's independent Ukraine lasted only a week. The Russians didn't change much… many of the faces were even the same.

At first, things were a bit chaotic, but chaos was good. Then stories of what was transpiring in Russia began. They didn't want to be called Russians any more, but Soviets. Reds. They asked for crops. Stefan was happy to oblige. Well, happy is an overstatement. It was a tax more reasonable than they remembered under the Empire.

Olga got to know this Jewish family, something of their traditions. That they didn't agree with the Orthodox patriarch, instead they thought Jesus hadn't come yet. Vanessa learned to add and subtract from Adam, and how to keep the finances for the farm. She heard about their families, in far off Poland. And some who were buried too soon in the black Ukraine earth.

Ten years passed, mostly prosperous years, but the stories about what was happening in Russia, "the Soviet Union," what was happening to the petty nobility, the merchants, to Jews.. and even to kulaks, like Stefan. The taxes grew greater.

Until finally, in 1928, Red Army Soldiers came. They wanted more than all the food. They wanted to take the Cossacks to forbidding places in Russia, take her family away from her land and away from God's graces. Stefan had taken crops to market. They hid the Jewish family. Mama sent Olya to the barn to collect eggs. When the screams came, Olya ran back to the window of the hut.

A dark haired woman was asking her mother about Stefan. When Mama didn't answer, the men cut Pavlo. Mama was proud, and spit on the woman. In a flash, this woman grasped Olga's youngest brother by the ankle and hurled him against the wall. There was a sickening crunch. Pavlo jumped at her, but one of the men with a pistol shot him. The other man shot Mama.

The dark haired woman turned to Mama's murderer. "Durak," she had said. Then she slapped him so hard his neck broke.

Adam gently placed his hand over Olya's mouth. He whispered, "come quietly, do you understand?" in Olya's ear. She nodded, and they scurried to the tree line.

They slept in one of the neighboring barns that night. In the morning, Adam returned with her father. "Princess," Stefan had said when he saw her. "Oh Princess."

They left for Warsaw that day. There were thousands of Jews on the road, but not many Kulaks. Rumors suggested most of the Kulaks were gathered on trains and shipped to Russia.

So Stefan and Olya Cossack considered themselves lucky indeed to be traveling West on foot, with a family that loved them. There was a dusty enclosure under the Great Synagogue in Warsaw that Stefan chose.

Olya stayed there with her father for several days, then with the Jewish family in a house with another family. When Stefan brought her back to the little basement room in the Synagogue, there were two boxes there. "What is this, Papa?" Olya asked Stefan, when she tasted the powder. Then there wasn't anything more to remember of that day.

Warsaw

It was hot. Very, very hot. Stefan opened his eyes and assessed his surroundings. "I am still in the box," he thought. Either the timer/lock has malfunctioned or something is very wrong.

He propped his feet against the lid, and placed both hands against it also. Then vigorously, Stefan popped the lid off the box and jumped into the inferno. He glanced around the crypt and saw Vanessa's box across the room. Grabbing a column, Stefan crushed the lock and flung open the box. Vanessa's eyes opened. "Hello princess," Stefan said. "Do you remember me?" he asked her.

"Papa?" She asked. He grabbed her hand, and together they ran.

Perhaps it was an accident that no one saw a 38 year old man, and his 14 year old daughter (at least from appearances). Perhaps the crowds were just too interested in watching the synagogue burn. Stefan saw the German uniforms but only realized what they were later.

He glanced around once from the burned apartment they had run to. Scissors, not very sharp ones. Some old clothing, but clean. Stefan cut Olya's hair to match his own. Removed the pretty embroidered dress and placed the baggy coat on her shoulders. She stepped into the trousers. They picked a hilltop with trees. Then walked to it. They kept walking until they saw refugees. Traded information. The Germans were fighting the Russians. Stefan considered the options. His Russian, and Olya's, was passable. Neither spoke German.

They walked until they found elements of the Polish Home Army, willing to work in any capacity in a Russian tank. The Soviet Armies didn't stop at Ukraine. Polish and Russian armies fought one another in the earthworks left after "The Great War." Stefan and Olya were fortunate to sleep through that conflict, waking early when the Germans invaded Poland and pushing Stefan and Olya into the Polish Home Army.

Although the Poles fought against Soviet Armies in 1920, when the Germans attacked the Soviet Union, Stefan, Olya and indeed the entire Polish Home Army were absorbed into the 1st Belorussian Front, allowing Stefan and Olya the opportunity to join the Russian 2d Tank Army (part of the Belorussian Front).

In mid-July 1944, the armies of the 1st Belorussian Front began to pressure German forces around Warsaw. Near Brest-Litovsk, Soviet armies threatened the German rail and communications center located there.

The Front was able to push the 4th Panzer army toward Siedlce and Lublin, ultimately encircling the German 2nd Army around Brest. Russian artillery subsequently prepared objectives for the 47th, 69th and 8th Guards Armies, which were able to penetrate thin German defenses remaining east of Kovel. Then on July

20th, one of the Tank Brigades of 11th Tank Corps (8th Guards Army) reported reaching the river Bug, cutting off a German retreat.

Ordered that night to move out towards Bug, Stefan's 2nd Tank Army (under the command of Lieutenant General Bogdanov) reached the western end by noon on July 21st. and subsequently attacked, first towards Lublin and then north-west toward Pulawy and Deblin.

One day their sergeant from the Polish Home Army announced that the 2d Tank Army needed reinforcements. Named for a famous Polish pianist, who lived most of his life in Paris (you should visit his museum in Warsaw, if you ever go there), Sergeant Chopin introduced Stefan and Olya to their new sergeant, Alexander Scriabin Vodka.

Sergeant Vodka announced proudly, "The Russian T-34 is the best tank in the world," which unfortunately wasn't true by 1944. He went on, "The T-34 is 26 tons heavy and 22 feet long. It has a 76.2mm main gun, a coaxial 7.62 machine gun and a front mounted 7.62 bow machine gun."

He smiled at his two new recruits. "Our tank has a four-man crew. This is our driver, Private Putin." Putin waved. Vodka continued, "I am the team chief/loader. We need a gunner, who operates the main gun and coaxial machine gun, and a bow machine gunner. Which do you want to be?"

Stefan and Olya exchanged glances. "I will be your gunner," said Stefan. "Okay Mr. Bow Gunner," Sergeant Vodka said to Olya, grabbing her arm, "Private Putin will show you how the machine gun works." She climbed into the tank. Stefan climbed in after her.

Sergeant Vodka showed Stefan how to operate the main gun and the coaxial machine gun. "The new Front Commander has given us a day's rest. We are attacking Radzymin tomorrow." They slept in the tank that night. Putin offered Olya some of his vodka. She took a swig, but he wasn't that generous. Otherwise, the smell in the tank was unpleasant and the seat relatively uncomfortable. She tried to fall asleep, finally drifting off to the sound of her father's quiet conversation with Sergeant Vodka.

She woke to the sound of a tank engine in her ear. She glanced at Putin, who raised his eyebrows, as he put the tank in gear. She peered through her site, watching Polish Home Army soldiers walking on the side of the road, and another T-34 just ahead on the road.

There was a whining sound, and the tank just ahead exploded. The Home Army troops scattered into the woods and machine gun bullets scattered dirt around them, then pinged into the hull.

Olya glanced at Putin, who raised his eyebrows again. "I think I know what happened to the previous gunner," she thought. They pulled around the burning hull in front of them and continued forward.

Suddenly off to the side they saw German tanks. Were they Panthers or Tigers? Who knew? But they were shooting, and Olya shot back. "Concentrate on the infantry with that," shouted Putin. "You are just wasting bullets shooting at the tanks."

Just then, the main gun went off. Of course, she was sure her father was a good aim, and there was a flash on one of the tanks. But when the dust cleared, the tank was moving toward them as if nothing happened. There was no gap between the flash of that Tiger's main gun and a ferocious explosion just behind her.

Olya blinked and shook her head, hoping the ringing in her ears would go away. 25 feet away, her father jumped to his feet. There was no sign of Putin or Vodka. Stefan grabbed her hand, saying "Good thing we are vampires," and ran forward with her, into a tree line.

That night they found one of the battalion commanders in the 8th Guards Tank Corps. Stefan found a job in another T-34, filling a TC/loader vacancy. Olya was told to drive one of the "mortar" trucks.

In those days, no one was allowed to call the BM-13 Katyusha multiple rocket launch truck it's real name.

Multiple rocket launchers weren't very accurate, and took 50 minutes to reload. But they were mobile, devastating, and perhaps most important, cheap to make, so there were a lot of them. The Soviets considered the name classified until after the war.

The 8th Tank Corps took near and far side banks of the river Vistula but lots of tanks exploded. When they talked later, Stefan bragged about driving alongside a few German tanks, orchestrating some well-placed "main gun" shots which caused them to explode.

But far more T-34's exploded during those days, unfortunately. In aggregate numbers, almost half of the tanks in the 2d Tank Army were destroyed.

Olya wasn't sure what her rockets hit, after they launched. But she and the others in her truck never stopped moving, loading, shooting, moving, loading and shooting.

Later, people would say the XXXIX Panzer Corps won the battle of Radzymin. It was true, that the Russians lost more tanks and weren't able to take Warsaw back.

But at that time in the war, Germany could scarcely afford to lose even the lesser number of tanks they lost.

At the end of the war, Stefan and Olya found one another. But they never found Adam or any members of his family.

It was in the YMCA in Warsaw that Sessai found Stefan and a new protégé, Olya. Perhaps the best place for three ex-Pats to stay. The best place for a seventeen year old girl to grow out her hair, take the bindings off her chest, and try to be something of a joyful child.

There was a piano in the YMCA. Wojciech could play it. He didn't stick with the beat, although the beat was admittedly there, running at a feverish pace. Wojc just chose to delay his finger strikes on the keys, just beyond where the beat fell. Skowronski could play the drums. There were saxophone players, trumpet players. What was the name of the bass player?

It wasn't every night that they had a dance, but there were several. On the morning before such a dance, Stefan found his daughter and presented a gift. She opened it, then beamed. A bright blue dress. "Try it on," he said.

That night the Soviet State Jazz Band played. The leader, a Jewish trumpet player, named Ady Rosner, kept the music coming. Someone knew some dances… waltzes, swing steps.

Two or three young men danced with Olya. They stumbled through the steps, getting better, learning to move with one another, across the floor. The man in the Red Army uniform, sitting in the corner, was dour, however. Stefan saw him. So did Sessai.

The next morning, the three left the YMCA for a coffee shop. Pastries and coffee. Working clothes, not dresses.

"We have decided you and Sessai must go to New York." Stefan said. If he hadn't been able to find

Adam, he had been able to secure passage, train and boat, to New York City.

Olya didn't want to go, at least not right then. "At least, let me go back for the dress," she said. "There are plenty of dresses in New York City," was Sessai's response. "Why aren't you going with us, Papa?" Olya pleaded. "My place is in Ukraine," Stefan replied. "Our people need me, and my farm is calling for me." Olya frowned, staring at Sessai. "Why can't I go with you?" she asked her father. "It isn't safe," he answered. That was all.

"When will I see you again, Papa?" Olya asked. "I don't know," Stefan replied. "I don't know."

After breakfast they walked to the rail head, where many other civilians were boarding a train. Olya and Sessai boarded. Stefan waved as the train began its chugging trip to Le Havre, France. Then he melted into the crowd and began his slow trip back to Ukraine.

There was no time for small talk. "here, your very own English-Russian dictionary. I'm sorry, no

Ukrainian-English, but it's close enough." Sessai and Olya reviewed phrases she might need, such as "family in Kansas," and "it has been a difficult war."

##

After they arrived in Le Havre, Sessai found American Army uniforms. It wasn't hard to find the name of someone who wasn't going home. "Vanessa Smith" was what her papers said. Sessai smiled. "It's a pretty name."

They joined the crowd boarding the SS Sea Robin. Passage took seven days.

Vanessa

How old is a wreck when you see it off the side of the road? If you didn't see a car meander, or dart to avoid a deer, and there is no steam or smoke, no person outside, examining the results, you might not notice. You will assume it had been sitting there for some time. Perhaps there were even a few passersby that evening.

That farmer should not have been driving down that road at that time. Initially, he just passed that little blue Toyota. But he got to thinking, "It wasn't there when I passed here earlier," so he went back. Even got out… and saw the blonde girl wedged between the air bag and her seat.

There were no skid marks on the road, only tire marks in the soil. Of course, even after the wreck had been cleared away, the flesh of the tree was exposed where the bumper and hood made impact. The broken glass would eventually absorb into the ground, but not for almost six months.

The farmer who stopped to call 911 thought he saw a man in his headlights when approaching, but when he got out to see, there was only a young woman trapped between the air bag and her seat. The woman was unconscious. The ambulance took a few moments to arrive.

In any event, the farmer should not have been there. He should have been home with his wife already, not on the way home from his lover. So he wasn't very observant and didn't give his name because he didn't want to get caught. Silly, because his lover was actually his wife's lesbian lover, so everyone knew about his sins. Only, he didn't know they knew. They were scheming to take his farm, which had been in his family for centuries. His wife had lost interest in him shortly after the marriage. The farmer didn't notice that either, but then, men will always think they strayed, won't they?

##

She opened her eyes, then squinted. It was bright in the room. She glanced around. White sheets, blue pillow cases, blue blankets, blue gauze "outer" curtains (how pretty, she thought sarcastically) with thick white inner curtains. There were wires attached to her arm, attaching her to a rather large beeping thing. This thing was on wheels.

Near it was a table, also on wheels. She gazed at a magazine sitting on the table. "Newsweek" with a picture of some matronly women. The door opened. Chatter between a woman and a man. They glanced at her, and immediately both smiled. "She's awake" the woman said. "Welcome back," said the man. Who are these people, she wondered.

They pulled seats next to her bed and began talking nonstop. About college next week, driving to Baltimore. About the fencing coach. About how excited everyone was to have a woman in the aeronautics department. She was silent. Amazed.

"I'm sorry." she said. "I don't remember anything."

##

Everyone was very understanding. The accident had been violent, she was lucky to be alive. Her memory will come back, they said. So traveling to college was quite surreal. Arriving, she wondered, "I chose this?" Her bags went to her room, her parents (the man and woman) cried tears when they said good bye. She hugged them and told them she loved them. Who are they, she kept wondering. Bill and Julie from Kansas. Yes, but how is it I don't remember them? Vanessa wondered.

"I'm Cammie, your roommate. Can't wait for fencing to start!" said the girl who was in the room when they and the things arrived, while Mom and Dad were there. After the goodbyes, Cammie was quick to itemize the parties in store for the weekend and the schedule for the next few days. "Lots of tours and social stuff. Kind of geeky, but, maybe fun."

Vanessa nodded. "Wow," she thought, with a sigh. Cammie smirked, "I heard about the accident. Are you okay?"

"Thanks for asking about it. I seem to be fine physically, but I can't remember anything." The phone in her pocket rang… some pleasant face, a man, was calling. Vanessa touched the green button. "hey, what do you think? Great? Sorry I haven't seen you since you woke up. I came to visit a few times, but you were sleeping."

"I don't remember anything." She answered. "Oh, wow. They said that might happen. Uhh.. do you remember me?" asked the phone.

Vanessa glanced at Cammie, who was nonchalantly trying to ignore the conversation. "Not really. Sorry." The man was silent for a second. "Ohhh myyyy God. Ok. Well… I'm Tom. Your boyfriend. We agreed to see other people at college. I'm at Cornell. It's a long way away. But.. anyway, I miss you already and just wanted to say hi."

Cammie made a happy smile and shrugged. "Hi," said Vanessa. "Thanks for calling. It's pretty great, I think. My roommate seems great. Classes start in a few days. Maybe I'll call you after the first day. Is that okay?"

"Well," said Tom. "If you don't remember me, I guess you can't miss me, can you?" Vanessa laughed lightly. "I'm sure I will remember everything soon. That's what everyone says. Talk with you in a few days, okay?" His reply was upbeat "Okay. Love you, Miss you. Talk with you then." Then the line went dead.

Vanessa smiled at Cammie, who smiled back. "Shall we grab dinner?" she asked. "Sure." And off they went.

##

The first day of fencing, she even felt butterflies in her stomach. What will I remember, she wondered. She and Cammie stuck pretty much together, and made faces at the arrogance of the upper classman. During the brief skirmishes Vanessa had no trouble fending off all attackers.

During a break, a middle aged oriental man walked into the crowd of girls, the fencers, and tapped Vanessa on the shoulder. "A moment," he asked. "I like your technique." She looked at her colleagues, wondering who he was. It seemed a bit strange to be approached here, but then.. the past few days had been incredibly, and pretty much non-stop, strange.

"Thank you," she answered, following him to the wall at one side of the room.

"Vanessa, right?" He asked. "Yes. I'm sorry. I've had an accident, I don't remember any one."

"Ah. Well, that is quite normal." he replied. "My name is Sessai. I am here to give you a bit of advice. I won't be here to keep reminding you, so you need to listen and… follow my advice."

Vanessa shrugged. Bill and Julie from Kansas hadn't said anything about a Sessei. "You are an unusual girl," the man went on. "More unusual than you can imagine. When you are ready, I will tell you all about it. But for the time being, just a bit of advice."

"Okay, what is it," Vanessa asked, glancing at the rest of the team, who were headed to the weight room. "First, you are very strong. Don't let anyone see that. You will be tested in a few minutes, keep everything to a few bars above the weakest woman. Maintain those results for your entire career here. Do you understand." The man had a very serious look about him.

"Whatever," Vanessa replied. "Typical teenager, you don't believe me. Then do this. After practice today, after every one has gone, return to the weight room. Place the bench press machine at twice the weight of the strongest tested girl today. You won't have trouble lifting it. But you cannot, under any circumstances, show others your strength." He nodded at her, solemnly. "Understand?" He asked. "Sure," she responded. Laughing to herself: double the strongest girl. She was relatively certain who that would be. A bull of a girl.

Sensei continued. "Here is my email. After you graduate, because of your scholarship, you will serve in the Army. You may come visit me during leave, in your second year of the Army, or wait until your commitment there is fulfilled. If you wait until after your commitment, however, you may stay with me for as long as you want. I have much to teach you." She glanced at him, thinking that it would all make more sense when she remembered but also considered that this Sessei might simply be a mad old man that wandered in off the street. On second thought, he knew her name. "Umm. Okay." She glanced at the crumpled paper in her hand, an email address and a "snail mail" address. "I live in Mikawa, Japan." The man said, as he scurried off.

Vanessa jogged to the weight room. Others were being tested. She watched them all and followed Sessei's instructions. One of the seniors, Carol, lifted the most weight on the bench press.

She followed everyone up the stairs, then carefully retraced her steps after seeing Cammie talking with one of the other freshmen, and the coaches occupied with upper classmen.

Vanessa walked immediately to the bench press machine and set it at twice Carol's winning weight. She gazed at the stack and lay down under the bars. She shook her head as she positioned her hands on the bar, then easily lifted the weight to arm lock height. She did two more repetitions, then stopped, replacing the weight. "How is this possible?" she wondered. She set the pin at half again as heavy and performed another repetition.

Again, no effort. "Wow." Vanessa mumbled. "I wonder what I'm going to learn next…."

##

Squeak, squeak, tap, tap. Scratch, scratch, tap, squeak. A tall red haired "TA" (teaching assistant, typically PhD candidate) was filling the board with mathematical symbols. They were hieroglyphics. The words that came from his mouth after he finished most of the scrawl… weren't that helpful either.

There were more hieroglyphics, interspersed with verbal interjections like, "It intuitively follows…," when mostly, it didn't intuitively follow. Vanessa pondered her options, ultimately concluding, "I'm going to learn this."

##

She glanced at Cammie, thinking how nicely she cleaned up. More fencing practices together, shared meals, dorm room dialogs. And walking up Saint Paul Street, talking options.

"Fredrick likes you," Cammie was saying, referring to one of their dorm mates.

"Really, I don't think so," Vanessa replied. "I really like your make-up. Good job."

"Ha, ha, you are changing the subject."

"Fredrick is a geek. Ok, his nose is kind of cute, but I don't think that's going to work out."

They passed the tennis courts five minutes ago. The baseball stadium was passing now. Cars zipping past, the ripping sounds of tires against pavement.

The streets weren't packed with pedestrians, but they weren't the only passers-by.

"How popular are these parties," Vanessa asked, again attempting to change the subject.

"They get pretty popular once people are done studying." Ten pm was early still. But they had agreed they would get an early start, leaving the party just after twelve. "We will probably be leaving just as things are heating up."

Vanessa wondered if that was a good idea. Ultimately, she decided it was. There will be plenty of time to enjoy watching fellow classmates make fools of themselves later this year, maybe even later this month. Practice starts early tomorrow….

##

"You are lucky to have survived," Sessai told Vanessa.

"Where are my Mom and Dad," Vanessa asked. "Where am I?"

"We weren't planning to make the substitution yet, but you really gave us no choice."

"What are you talking about? Where are my parents?" She asked, in reply.

"Would you like to see them? We can't let you talk to them, but we can drive past the house."

"What do you mean I can't talk with them? Is this some kind of human trafficking incident? I'm going home…" Vanessa glanced at Sessai, wondering about him, her aching head and this disconcerting set of assertions the old man was making.

"You aren't who you think you are," he replied.

"What's that supposed to mean?"

"Do you recognize this person?" Sessai responded, handing her a picture. Vanessa glanced at it. Then glanced back at Sessai. "It's me," she said.

"Actually, it's not. You are her clone."

"A clone. You mean like the sheep?"

"Well, actually, a vampy. You are her vampy, created from her almost twenty years ago. Relatively simple procedure, thanks to Julie's in vitro egg thing. Bill and Julie don't even know there are two of you."

"Two of us. What?"

"We are calling you Olya Cossack, at this point. The person in that picture, we are calling her Vanessa Smith. She is on her way to Hopkins with Bill and Julie, in a few days. We are taking you to Europe."

"Europe?"

"You were at a party. Drinking a lot. Telling everyone you were quitting fencing and dropping out of Hopkins. Something about spending a year in Europe. You had a big argument with Tom. You know, your boyfriend Tom? Then you stormed out… shouldn't have been driving, but managed to get the car going the correct direction, then ran it into a tree."

"My boyfriend Tom," she muttered, placing a hand to her head.

"I placed your twin Vanessa in the wreck and brought you here. You have been unconscious until now."

"I'm not sure if my head hurts from the car wreck or the bullshit you're feeding me."

"It's going to take a while for you to absorb all this, and to see I'm telling you the truth. Vanessa is about a hundred years old. She has just completed a sixty year.. well.. what we call a sleeping. She won't remember your life with Bill and Julie, because you lived that, she didn't. And frankly, Vanessa won't remember her earlier life either, for a time. Everyone will blame the accident for her memory loss."

"Wait. So.. some other person gets to go to Hopkins instead of me, gets my ROTC scholarship instead of me. Even gets my name? What is this bullshit Olya Cossack name?"

"You wanted to go to Europe. You were the one who got in the traffic accident. You really left us no alternative but to work the substitution. So here we are."

"Europe. I do remember.. it was so much. Calculus all summer. Fencing. No break. And off to Hopkins.

God. So…," Olya glanced at Sessai, "Okay, I guess. When do we go? When can I see my Mom, my parents, again?"

"We might be able to arrange some calls with your Mom. But remember, they think Vanessa is you. For the time being, you need to rest. I have some errands I need to take care of. I will see you in a week." With those words, Sessai unceremoniously stood and left the room, locking it as he exited.

"A week," Olya pondered, glancing around the room. She saw a pair of jeans and shirt folded on a chair in the corner, and saw an air duct screen near the roof in a corner of the room. After changing into the jeans and shirt and confirming the door was, indeed, locked, Olya moved the chair under the air duct, pried the screen off with hardware from her bed and climbed into the duct. Moments later she had pushed the air conditioner to the ground at the other end and dropped to the ground.

A couple miles away was a diner. Can you imagine, a "Servers wanted," sign on the door? Olya contemplated the people she knew from High School, and thought of a girl who planned to stay in the area, and was starting at the University of Kansas in the Fall. "Can you start today," they asked, after she applied for the job using Karen's name.

Olya (Karen? Vanessa?) flirted with everyone who came in to the diner that day. Even the women. Her smiles and twinkling eyes earned her several nice tips and one annoyed Mother. It also inspired the interest of the scum bag married man who slipped his ring into his pocket upon entry of the diner.

"When do you get off," he had asked. She told him five. He agreed to take her to dinner.

"This is risky," she thought, getting into his car a few hours later. But she smiled sweetly at him while they drove to the Japanese restaurant. She knew all the Japanese restaurants in the area, but hadn't been to this one in a few years. They had a pleasant enough conversation for most of the meal, until he started alluding to some rather pornographic interests.

She squinted at him and contemplated options. "I have to meet a friend at the mall, to buy a birthday gift for my Mom. But maybe we can get together tomorrow. Do you usually come to the diner for lunch?"

"Tomorrow is bad for me. Thursday?"

"Sure. But…" Vanessa glanced into his eyes. She never understood the cheating thing, but knew how guys always fell for that glance. "… can you do me a big favor. I need to borrow two hundred dollars to buy that gift for my mom. I'll pay you back on Thursday."

He gave her two hundred dollars from his wallet. "Don't worry about it," he had said. "See you Thursday," were his words when he left her at the mall. "Thanks," she replied, with absolute sincerity.

Olya watched the married man drive away, then walked down the sidewalk past the mall to the Greyhound bus station. "One way to Ithaca, New York," she said to the portly lady at the ticket window. After receiving her ticket, Olya walked onto the platform to wait for her bus to Cornell.

##

"Mr. Sessai," Vanessa said as he approached.

"Just Sessai, please. But this isn't about me." This guy always has a grim expression on his face, Vanessa thought. "We have a problem."

"We? What problem?" Vanessa asked.

"Any feedback for me from the weight room?" he asked her.

"You were right," Vanessa responded. Sessai nodded. "I'm going to give you the short version of this story. There will be plenty of time to talk details later. First, you are about a hundred years old, but slept most of the past sixty. The person that Bill and Julie Smith raised is your clone, a girl named Olya Cossack." Sessai glanced at her incredulous expression. "You will eventually remember your life, but you will remember a childhood in Ukraine, fighting in World War II and dancing in Warsaw. You will remember New York City in the '40's, but you will never remember your childhood with Bill and Julie, because you didn't live it. Olya did."

"What?"

"I am here to tell you this. To fill in any details you'd like about your life with Bill and Julie, because you need to behave the loving daughter with them. But I also have a problem. Olya has escaped."

"Olya. You mean me?" Sessai smiled and replied, "Olya went to a party the night of your auto accident. She had been feeling overwhelmed. Sword instruction at the Five Rings club, calculus to prepare for school. And here was the end of the summer already. She told everyone she was quitting and stormed out of the party, drunk. After that she crashed the car into a tree. I put you in the car and took Olya to medical care. I spoke with Olya when she woke from her coma and answered lots of questions. That was a week ago."

"Calculus. God. I'm totally overwhelmed."

"Understandable. Talk about that with Julie. The accident is an excellent excuse. She will have ideas."

"And other than the strength thing and some amazing quickness, I am, like, the worst swords person on the team. They are all pretty shocked that I am even there."

"I taught you a lot of swordsmanship in New York City. Before you consciously remember things, your body will remember the swordsmanship. The Calculus is another story. You are remarkably intelligent, but there are things that you don't know, that everyone thinks you know. Things the accident will excuse for a while, but ultimately, things you will need to learn, fresh, and understand well. Like calculus."

"Okay," Vanessa said quietly, in response. Sessai went on, "I need to know about Tom, your boyfriend. Olya's boyfriend. Have you spoken with him?"

"He called me the other day. I told him I didn't remember anything."

"Of course. That's all?" Vanessa responded, "yes."

Sessai asked for Tom's phone number. "Do you have his address?" He asked her.

Vanessa pulled out the phone and gave Sessai what she had about Tom, including his phone number. Then she asked, "You say I am a hundred years old. How is that possible? What am I?"

"I hesitate to use the word. So much false, fairy tale, mumbo jumbo."

Vanessa's eyebrows went up. "Concentrate on being a competent student, then a good one. Stay credible in ROTC. Get to know Bill and Julie, be a good daughter. Make some friends," Sessai said.

"You are avoiding the question," Vanessa interrupted. Sessai shrugged. "You are a vampire," he answered. "Don't bite anyone."

##

Sessai left her in the coffee shop and wandered across campus. He had parked on a side street between a hearse and a truck. He popped the lock, opened the door and lowered himself into the seat. He keyed the Cornell address into the positioning system and pondered travel options. "A long trip. Perhaps take two days for this one." He pulled into traffic, heading north.

##

"Someone wanted you," her boss said. Olya glanced where the boss was pointing. "Oh shit," Olya thought. "My dad," she told her boss.

"Oh really," was the response. "He said he's your uncle. Whatever."

Great. Some story fixing to do. Olya slid into the booth opposite Sessai. "You found me," was all she said. He looked at her and sighed. "What have you done?"

"Spent some time with my boyfriend. You are an asshole," she replied.

Sessai smirked. "Do you want to stay here or go to Europe? Presumably Tom is calling you Vanessa."

"Yes, Tom calls me Vanessa. At this point he thinks I've gone back to Hopkins. We can go to Europe. This place sucks." Olya was abrupt. Concise. Incredibly cute. Evidently she had absorbed her situation.

"I don't know how your new Vanessa can possibly do the course work at Hopkins. Or fence on that team. It would have been a stretch for me, and Julie has been driving my skills for years."

"She's a talented girl," was all Sessai would say. "Have you signed a lease?"

"No. Month to month thru Craig's List."

"Okay. Give notice here and with your landlord. We leave for Europe on Saturday."

A Nurse

Isis arrived in Springfield, Illinois, in 1839.

She met Mary Todd at a political event. The two were together interested in funding politicians. Mary was talking with great animation about her suitors, both candidates for the Senate. Isis suggested Steve Douglas. Mary chose the other candidate.

A year after the Civil War began, Mary invited Isis to attend a party. Her husband, recently elected President, was expressing concern about the stability of the Union after they won the war. "An eternal optimist," she had said.

"Oh, we will win the military conflict. But will we win the peace?" he wondered. He specifically expressed concerns about rebel heroes. "Men like Stonewall Jackson," he said.

Isis raised her eyebrows. "I might know someone who can help you with that problem. There is a nurse working at Campbell General Hospital, who knows talented assassins. Give her $10,000 and she will make arrangements." The man pulled on his beard. "I'm not comfortable with assassinations."

"Your choice. Probably fewer casualties in the war, and certainly less conflict after it is over, however. Just use the words 'Deux ex Machina' when you meet her and she will trust you."

It was the President's first visit to the hospital. Cleo was surprised when he asked to talk with her in private. Of course, she consented, but was shocked when he handed her the envelope and said the words, "Deux ex Machina."

She examined the contents of the envelope and looked back at his haggard face. "Stonewall Jackson," was the only other thing he said. Cleo stood and left the hospital.

##

Reporting to Chimborazo. Claiming to be new to nursing. Helped a bit after the boys were hurt at Bull Run. "Which one?"

"Both," she replied. There was plenty of work. They asked her to do it. Many of her patients arrived without a firearm. Enough had one for her to collect two Bridesburg muskets and a Remington 1861 pistol.

The Bridesburgs were .58 caliber, muzzle loading, single fire rifles. The Remington was .44 caliber with six chambers. She fired all three in the woods on her first day off. Satisfied, she hid her tools in a box not far from the hospital, and ran into a burial detail before dinner on Sunday.

Of course, the coroner was dressing several recently departed in dress uniforms. Cleo discretely gathered matching top and bottom field uniforms for washing. One pair of trousers were ruined from a bullet to the hip (blood and torn cloth), the other from a bullet through the heart; keeping a complete set was too much trouble.

Cleo put them on. Studied whether the visor to the right or left was best. Heading to Chancellorsville, Cleo was confident she appeared the part of the soldier. Hiding a second musket was a bit uncomfortable, although the 1861 revolver went easily into her pack.

"Sir, I have been told to serve with the Valley District." He asked for her orders, then passed her from one sergeant to another when she didn't have them. After inspecting her rifle, they assigned her to a squad. Someone was talking about Stonewall Jackson. Everyone was hypothesizing about an upcoming battle, although details were scarce.

Then one day Jackson and his staff rode past. Jackson held his arm up in the air (one of the men said Stonewall had one arm longer than the other, so always held one up to improve circulation). "That's pretty distinctive," thought Cleo.

In the chaos of Chancellorsville, Cleo slipped away and slung her second Bridesburg around her shoulder.

She stuck the Remington in her belt and walked for high ground. There were shouts. Challenges and passwords. Finally, in the dusk and smoke, Cleo saw the shadow with the arm in the air.

Riding Little Sorrel, the chestnut gelding, with group of officers, returning from battle. Cleo aimed the first Bridesburg at the arm, dropping the rifle after her shot. The arm was still up… had she missed? She fired again, dropping the second Bridesburg some twenty-five yards beyond the first.

Cleo drew the pistol and took a shot at Jackson's rein hand. The clamor began: someone saw the general had been hit.

Cleo went back to her little chest to gather her nurse's dress. She left the 1861 in that box with a few other items, then wandered back toward the battlefield. Someone said Stonewall had been brought to a local plantation.

It took her a few hours to find Stonewall Jackson at Thomas Chandler's Fairfield Plantation.

"Sir, they said there was need for a nurse here." They were all so tired. So grim. A hero was wounded.

Cleo added, "You can check with Doctor McCaw at Chimborazo. He would remember me."

She inspected the general, who was in relatively good spirits, finding two (of her?) shots hit the arm and his reign hand had also been hit. This was not the time for smiling. But she thought, "I haven't lost it."

Two days later the doctor attempted an amputation. Cleo casually severed an artery, although no one saw her motion or even the instrument that did the work. It wasn't long before the doctor realized that his patient would not survive. He blamed himself.

##

Wandering away from the plantation, Cleo wasn't certain she wanted to return to nursing work. Her box, undisturbed, had a humble set of clothing and the

Remington. Enough of the 10 thousand to last for some time. And her horned sphere dagger. Cleo gathered them and walked away. She thought she would keep walking until she found a hotel.

The proprietor invited her in after inspecting the bills she offered. He suggested she sit with another guest near the fire while they readied her room.

"Fancy seeing you again," said Isis.

"Yes, quite the fancy," replied Cleo. This meeting, of course, was no accident. "Your magic hasn't faded."

"Oh, I don't know about that," answered ISIS with a smile. I have a gift for you," she added, pointing to a wrapped item on the table. "You have done well, young princess."

Cleo cut the binding strings with her dagger, to reveal a sword. This time, instead of just a horned sun at the top of the handle, the base of the handle were stylized Egyptian wings, spread for flight.

"Fine German steel," said Isis. "The best in the world."

"What am I going to do with this," wondered Cleo aloud.

"A wall decoration, to discuss with your suitors," suggested Isis. "I don't want to discuss my love life with you or anyone else, goddess."

"What happened to my deferential, joyful princess?" wondered Isis. "You were so submissive and worshipful as a child."

"In those days I was a princess, with a Kingdom. Conspiring to seize control of a government from my arrogant, undeserving, brother, against the wishes of my all-powerful father. Today I am…" Cleo was seeking the best words, "… an individual contributor."

"Well," responded Isis, "you are tired. It has been an eventful week. In any event, this sword is more than a decoration. You need to understand that your kind know about you. They know you are alive, they just don't know where you are. They consider you a criminal. At some point, they will come for you."

"A criminal?" asked Cleo. "Well… thanks for that!"

"Oh," laughed Isis. "These little tasks I have helped you find are nothing. The Order probably has no idea you have been active in the affairs of the human race. But they consider your involvement with Caesar in Rome to be an unprecedented interference with humankind and an interference that has largely been considered a disaster."

"I don't remember that very well," said Cleo.

"Well, you need to refresh your understanding about making and training vampies. And you need to learn to use this sword. So, you can protect your pretty arched neck from being separated from your unusually strong shoulders."

"Perhaps we can talk again in the morning," said Cleo, when the innkeeper muttered that her room was ready.

"Perhaps," said Isis. "I think there is time."

##

Eggs, milk and biscuits. Cleo enjoyed an American breakfast. Isis swept into the room, "What a beautiful day," she said.

Picking at her sausages, Isis contemplated, "You know, for years I was the most popular goddess on earth. There would hardly have been time for your little troubles. Even had a few pure followers not too far from here, but things didn't turn out too well for them."

Cleo studied her benefactor, who went on. "Despite the pacifism of the founder, Christians can really be quite nasty. So, I mostly gain my recruits through a more Christian flavor, at least in this part of the world, or in Europe. Some would even say the Madonna is only a feeble imitation of my mother-earth aura, a longstanding inspiration to artists, musicians, peasants and governments to this day."

"What can you tell me about making vampies?" Cleo asked.

"You know, life is more than the practicalities. History, art, theology, you really ought to reengage with those."

Cleo responded, "I had enough of all that with my tutors, on my father's proverbial knee."

"Hardly," sniffed Isis, with disgust. "Perhaps we will enjoy a more interesting conversation next time. Vampies, yes, vampies. Presumably also learned on your father's knee."

Isis dabbed the corner of her mouth with a napkin. "They start with a bite. Many vampires choose to entice lovers this way. So much more cooperative than other vampires or mortals."

Cleo just listened.

"But within a month, perhaps as long after the first biting as a year, you must bite him," she smiled mischievously, "or her, again. Once is enough to achieve the desired effect, but many vampires enjoy feasting frequently."

"Feasting. I always avoided that. Was quite unbecoming of my brother."

"Yes. His proclivities became quite famous, didn't they?" Isis took another bite of her sausage, gazing at her clever little princess, then swallowing. "Well, in any event, princess practicality, you can create a squad, a legion or even an army of vampies. They of course don't have your strength, speed or reasoning, but they obey your will, which can be handy in a struggle with mortals in groups, and even with your own kind."

"A vampie can dispatch a vampire?" asked Cleo, genuinely curious.

"Well, only with a lot of luck. But they can be a very interesting distraction while you tend to your opponents in other ways." Isis nodded her head. "They can handle human weapons with training and dispatch numbers, even large numbers of humans with those, while distracting an opponent to serve up a head splitting or severing blow."

"I see," said Cleo. "Then I must also be wary of such distractions."

"Yes, you must," said the goddess.

##

After Isis went back to doing whatever goddesses do when they aren't absorbing praise or selecting wishes to grant among the admiring masses, Cleo contemplated options. "New York, I haven't seen New York in a while."

She found a coach that would take her there and found a boarding house near a fencing club. "Swordsmanship," she thought smiling. Pretending to be a man again, she learned the ins and outs of the various blades. "From what I have learned," she remembered, "cuts will be the most important strokes."

Parries and various distractions leading to a clean horizontal sweep just above and parallel to the shoulders. Blows glancing down from the ear. Upward flicks after a poke at a shoulder.

She left the sword from Isis in a box under the bed. She also abstained from recruiting vampies, at least for the moment.

##

"We wondered if it was true," said a short skinny man sitting next to a patient at Walter Reed. Words in Russian.

"What?" asked Cleo, subconsciously fingering her dagger.

"This ancient contact." The skinny man had a dour face. "The Russian head of state is a bit," he started to answer, scratching his chin, "doctrinally focused. Perhaps you can help us… become more pragmatic."

Cleo wondered if Isis was going to come up. "What are you doing here? How did you find me?"

"Does it matter? This is a Russian opportunity. You have worked for us before."

Cleo pondered a reply. "Perhaps," she answered. "But the price is $1M US dollars, with 50% paid up front." She produced a card with deposit instructions from her petticoat.

"That's fine," said the man, glancing at the card. "But it has to appear to be from natural causes."

"The target?"

"Vladimir Illyich Lenin."

"Okay. I initiate the operation upon deposit of your first 50%. The second 50% must arrive the day after his demise, or I will find you and your family."

"We are hard people to find. But that is no worry and no matter. The remainder will be paid upon demise."

Enough, she thought, turning abruptly and walking away. She went to see hospital leadership about a transfer to the Field Hospital in France. They had been asking for volunteers to go. When Cleo returned to check on her patient, the man was gone.

##

Her contact took her to Lenin's poison lab. Or was it Stalin's team there, working on instructions… from whom? Such a project may never be popular, but perhaps it was practical.

Years later Nikita Khrushchev would write about how paranoid Joseph Stalin was about being poisoned. Was he more knowledgeable about the topic than most, or was his paranoia the natural state for such an autocratic regime?

"Spiridon Ivanovich, meet our new maid," they said one day, introducing her to the cook. He was trusted, where she really was not.

But no matter. Several days later, Vladimir Illyich Lenin died of a massive stroke. There was a power struggle, but Stalin, the liaison to the intellectual font of the state, had an inside track.

Cleo said her good byes to Spiridon Ivanovich, who had become Stalin's trusted cook.

##

"They told me I might find you here," the mostly bald man said, after Cleo arrived in the headquarters tent of the Expeditionary Hospital. She had been summoned. It had been years, but mostly unremarkable years.

"I am honored sir."

He gazed at her with sad eyes. "Clearly we have a problem. A threat to our democracy. This conversation couldn't be delegated."

Cleo looked at the famous man without expression. "This was found in your quarters. It is yours?"

Cleo accepted the sun god dagger. "Yes," she answered, silently thankful he hadn't found the sword.

"If we don't stop him, George Patton will continue the war, and perhaps end democracy as we know it."

"I am a simple nurse, sir."

"That's not what Isis says."

"Isis? More Deux ex Machina?"

"Here is the number of your Swiss bank account and instructions for how to access the funds there. This is more important than your nursing work." He was matter of fact. Firm. Cleo stood, accepted the envelope, turned and left the tent.

"I will miss the work," she thought. Perhaps less lucrative at the other end of it, but work that comforts the heart. In addition to the account information, there was an address and enough bills in the envelope to cover local travel and probably secure passage across the Atlantic. What else might a woman want?

So many people in uniforms loaded in trains. Otherwise milling about. There was one walking a little dog. Amazing that no one was tending to his security. Perhaps he refused a security detail. She followed him for a time, and watched him open a door and walk inside.

She followed him off and on for a few days, contemplating options. One day, he jumped in front of a tram. That's what she said, but no one believed her. They called it an accident.

"Do you want this?" asked a woman. She had caught the little dog's leash. Cleo realized it was Isis.

"Well, no, I'm really a cat person," she replied.

"Somehow I guessed that about you."

"It's been a long time since we talked," said Cleo, in a bit of a sober mood.

"Yes. I guess you heard I was talking to the Russians about you."

"Yes, I concluded that. Wish you wouldn't."

Isis pursed her lips. "I won't find you any more work, princess. Frankly, I really didn't think you would last this long, even with the help from me."

"The order has no idea where to find me. Thanks for your advice."

"Well princess, I will never forget the prayers you devoted to me, when you were a little girl. Such prayers will take a person a long, long way."

"That's good to know," responded Cleo.

With a flash and puff of smoke, Isis was gone.

##

"Ma'am, we have a bit of an unusual request." Cleo wasn't happy to hear those words upon her first visit to her banker in twenty-five years.

She was stunned to hear the name, "Bobby Kennedy." Her Banker handed her a listing of her balance… exactly $5M higher than expected.

"Your customer assumes terms are the same as last time, with the exception that the amount has been increased to reflect inflation."

Cleo felt the first tremors of panic for two thousand years. "This conversation never happened." She veritably ran from the bank. Ducked into the train. Immediately transferred 50% of her balance to another bank. Then she walked to a news stand and bought every periodical and paper on it.

Within a day, she was sitting on a nondescript freighter for America, considering options. "Why Bobby Kennedy?" she wondered. "Should I accept?" There were no options for rejecting the assignment, although she thought she might transfer all but $5M from the account and instruct her banker to return that amount. Ultimately, she opted to keep the deposit and the assignment, but decided she would manipulate a new trigger.

Review of Bobby Kennedy's positions included strong anti-communism, progressive rights for United States citizens, alignment with "flower children" (Kennedy staffers hated all uniforms, be they military or law enforcement) and an interest in supporting the state of Israel. "Israel… our old slaves?" wondered Cleo.

So many years since her last visit to New York City. So many things had changed. Cleo thought about Isis's criticisms and thought she would visit the Village Theater for some music. A band called Cream, with a guitarist named Eric Clapton. In those days, Cleo didn't have much of an ear for music, but she liked what that man was able to do with a guitar.

Beatles music. A band called "The Grateful Dead." Jefferson Airplane. How can anyone be bored in this city, wondered Cleo.

She heard one of Bobby Kennedy's anti-communist colleagues was a hotel magnate, David Schine. That might be helpful, she thought. The Ambassador Hotel in Los Angeles, was owned by Schine, and famous for its jazz club.

In the outskirts of town, at a used car lot, Cleo bought a Karman Ghia Volkswagen. She bought some maps of the country and began her drive west.

At a little pawn shop in Kansas, Cleo bought a Savage/Stevens 22 caliber rifle. Some target practice to pass the day, after driving so many hours across such flat ground. An old skill, good as new.

Cleo decided the Israeli link was most interesting for her Bobby Kennedy task. After arriving in California, she enrolled in a popular Palestinian alma mater of the day, Hartnell College. She contemplated her romantic options… first considered in many, many, years.

In one class, a student raved against Israel. Evidently Israel's victory in the six-day war drove young Sirhan and his family the Old City of Jerusalem, a miserable place for a childhood. She smiled at him, and they had lunch. The Egyptian past was an interesting tie. Wasn't hard to direct his anger from general anti-Zionism to hi-profile Kennedy, who promised to send the Israeli's a bunch of US Phantom jets.

She thought about options. Street cars might be a challenge, she thought. Large caliber firearms are out of favor, she thought. 22 calibers are very accurate… and relatively quiet.

She and Sirhan traveled to Los Angeles in May. One day he showed her a 22 pistol he bought. "This guy is crazy," she thought, one night before heading to the Coconut Grove for a vodka. The guy who bought it … said his name was Cesar. "I have an affinity for that name," she said smiling, when he offered to buy her another. He was a security officer and liked the idea of working for the Kennedy campaign when they heard police weren't allowed to protect the candidate.

She found a little closet which shared a wall with the kitchen that night. A week later she cut a square hole at sitting height, then carefully reinserted the piece. It wasn't hard to insert a false ceiling and place her Savage/Stevens 22 in the space above.

Cleo wore her favorite polka-dot dress the night of Kennedy's California primary victory. She walked from the Coconut Grove with Sirhan, then whispered she forgot her coat. He glared at her… she knew he had his new pistol in his coat.

Cesar was on security staff and steered the Senator into the hotel kitchen.

With the commotion around the candidate in the kitchen, no one noticed her, even with the blue polka dots. She removed the rifle from the ceiling cavity and sat in her supported firing position. She pulled out the piece she had cut from the wall and gazed through the scope, waiting for her moment.

Just as the firing started, Kennedy stepped into her observation window. Cleo squeezed off two rounds toward a point behind Kennedy's ear, replaced the wall segment and returned the rifle to the ceiling cavity. She left her little closet and walked out of the hotel, never to return.

The second five million arrived in her account the next day. She arrived in London the following week.

Five Rings

"Big box," said Cammie. "Open it!" They were both studying the box in the middle of the dorm room. Inside there were four wooden swords. A book, "Five Rings." Then a second book, "Swordsmanship for women."

"Who is it from?" wondered Cammie. Vanessa shrugged, but took the book and set it on the table beside her bed.

##

Olya opened the door. "Hi." Sessai smiled. "May I come in?" She stepped out of the way and he walked into the small living room, almost stumbling over the cracked coffee table onto the threadbare couch.

Sessai turned to face Olya and pulled tickets from his coat pocket. "Here are tickets to Brussels. Do I need to chaperone you onto the airplane or can you handle getting to the airport?"

Olya took the tickets. Departure from Boston Logan. "I can get a bus." Sessai nodded. "Do you want to pick your apartment in Brussels or shall I do it for you?"

"Who is paying the rent?" Sessai folded his arms. "I will find you a job. Will also open a bank account for you there, since you need an address to do that. But you will need to pay your rent from your salary."

"I will pick the place. When will I see you again?"

"We can meet for dinner the day you arrive. I'll give you your bank account information and walk you through the new job. Here is a phone with a Brussels phone number." Sessai handed her a cheap Alcatel smart phone. "Chip is already installed. You can take that out and install another one in the event you'd like to use it here." Sessai managed a small smile. "In a lot of ways this is a great situation."

Olya thought for a minute. "So it's okay if I call my mom and Tom? What about Karen?"

Sessai chose his words carefully. "Your Mom and Vanessa are making a relationship. Vanessa needs her help to get through the first year. Probably best if you don't talk with her." Sessai paused for a moment. "Vanessa has no attachment to Tom, but that might be… awkward. What happened between you?"

Olya pulled a stool opposite Sessai, who was sitting on the threadbare couch. "My weekend with Tom was more intense than… any experience we had dating in high school. And… he has a roommate."

"A room mate?" Sessai asked. Olya's response: "I don't want to talk about it."

"Who is Karen?" he asked her. "I used Karen's name to get the waitress job in Kansas, and used it here also."

"Ingenious," was his response. "I would just let that go. Oh.. here is a Belgium passport.. Olya." She opened the passport. "I don't read German," she responded. "You're an expat. Your father, Stefan Cossack, is a Belgian citizen of Ukraine extraction.

You can be honest with people… you were raised by nice friends of the family in Kansas. If anyone asks for names, just say you'd rather not talk about it."

Sessai continued. "The job requires a fluent English speaker. We will have you studying Russian, but that can wait."

"Russian?" Olya was curious. Sessai answered, "We hope you can get proficient in a year or so, then we will move to Belorussia. Everyone speaks Russian in Eastern Europe."

"Belorussia… is that where I meet this supposed Dad?"

"No. You will meet Stefan in Brussels, probably when we meet for dinner. He arranged for the job."

"Job. What, am I a stripper?"

"Olya, this isn't a human trafficking incident. Your job is administrative, but we really need your help. You can study aeronautics after work, if you'd like. When you're ready. But this is an open book for you. We need your help for a few years, mostly 9 to 5, so you can knock off some coursework if that's of interest. Or just focus on learning Russian. Join the local fencing club or just join a gym. Apply to colleges in Europe or the US, really is up to you. We will produce some nice high school records for you. Very few people have the opportunity to redesign life the way you do."

"What if I want to work as a stripper? I hear its good money." Olya deadpanned. Sessai wasn't sure if she was serious. "Olya, you need a clearance to work for NATO, so the stripping job will need to wait a year or two. Your salary should be adequate for reasonable needs."

"Am I allowed to date?" Sessai's response: "Sure."

She reviewed her ticket and the passport, glancing at Sessai then back at her papers. "Okay, see you on October 10th. Guess you will text me the address of the restaurant?"

"Sure." After a few minutes of silence, Sessai stood and left the apartment.

##

Olya glanced at the tall man in the dark pilot's uniform. She was happy Sessai indulged her in first class tickets for the trip but was still a bit bored. "Hey sir, can I ask you a question?" she asked.

The pilot gazed at the pretty blonde and the empty first class seat next to her, on the aisle. "Sure," he answered.

Olya took a deep breath. "Is there truth to that mile-high club thing?" The pilot glanced at the stewardess responsible for first class, then sat next to Olya. "What do you want to know?" he asked, smiling, suspecting a memorable flight might be in store. He was surprised and impressed when he learned she had planned to study aeronautics at Hopkins.

##

Later, she gave him her number, not expecting a call. The next few weeks were a blur. Meeting Stefan Cossack and Taigen Sessai for dinner after arriving in Brussels. Starting work at NATO headquarters in Brussels. Studying Russian and meeting her Ukrainian tutor. Selecting and furnishing an apartment. Thinking about future options. Mostly avoiding men. Until the phone rang.

"Olya, it's Fred Clancy. Calling to arrange for Mile High club dues." She could hear his smile over the phone and took a deep breath. "When are you coming to Brussels?" She wondered. "It's taken a while to arrange, but for this weekend. Are you available?" This is sweet, she thought. Some might consider the age difference a bit of a scandal, but it was working for her. "I have a busy schedule" she lied, "but I can rearrange things. Shall I collect you at the airport or do you want to just come to my apartment?"

"Probably easiest if I just come to the apartment." Yeah, she thought, fewer complications. She gave him her address.

##

She wasn't sure what his expectations would be after the time in the cockpit. She wasn't sure what her expectations were, given how much older he was. The contrast to the weekend in Cornell was remarkable, however. "There are substantial benefits to an older man," Olya thought that Sunday morning as she brought him coffee and a scone, breakfast in bed.

"This is a surprise," he responded with a quiet smile. "You have been a nice surprise too," she responded. "I wasn't expecting to ever hear from you again." He pulled her firmly to him, then sipped his coffee. "You are quite a catch, if that's something you were wanting to be," was his response.

"I'm not sure what I want, but a gentleman caller is.. rather romantic. Do you think you will be coming to Brussels often?" She considered how lucky she was, to have stumbled across this decent, if somewhat adventurous, man. Others might have been much more unpleasant, even dangerous. Of course, at this stage, she was certain Stefan or Sessai would come to her rescue, should a rescue be in order.

"Might be easier for you to come to me." He glanced at her. "I can get you free tickets, when there is availability." Hmm, she thought. "I will have to give that option some thought. Can I pick where we meet?"

"Hmm. Within reason, I guess. New York. Atlanta. Chicago. Maybe even London."

Olya thought of her clone, who she had never met. "Baltimore?" she asked. He paused. Smiled. "Yes, we can do Baltimore."

##

"I hear you know a few things about flying."

Olya glanced up at her boss, Deputy Chairman of NATO's military committee. "Well, sir, can't claim I have thousands of hours as pilot in command, but I've got a pilot's license and am planning to study aeronautics."

He nodded. "Taking a break?"

Olya smiled. "A rare opportunity to spend a few years in Europe. I'm working on advancing my higher math skills and understanding this byzantine organization." Shessler smiled. "Let me know if you figure it out."

Olya was a few hours away from a long weekend in Baltimore. Six months to accrue the vacation and "good will" to get away. She glanced out the window. Not a bad view of Brussels. Shessler had eased into the role without fanfare, just as he had just walked past her desk into his office.

##

She smiled as she contemplated the introduction to her "twin." Her interview at Norma Jeans was scheduled for Saturday. They had told her she would begin work that night. Olya had found an exotic wardrobe shop close to the airport and had the phone number for the frat social committee chair where the lacrosse team were (mostly) members.

Then she placed a call for a cab. "Yes, to the airport." She stood, walked to the closet where she had stowed her carry-on.

##

The interview had gone well. The manager liked her "look" and agreed to give free entrance to the first ten from the frat she invited. She was up on stage for the first time, under the burning lights, though she wasn't sure whether the heat she felt was from them or the flush color red she turned taking her clothes off for the first time.

"These boys are enraptured," she thought, as one, then another, folded a dollar in her G-string, staring at her subtle, firm shape.

She smiled at the tall one with black hair, flirting with her eyes. "Team captain?" she wondered. One of the others whispered in his ear. His eyebrows went up and he glanced at her face. "Vanessa?" he asked. She bent down, patted him on the cheek, then walked into the dressing room.

"Mission accomplished," she thought, slipping on her jeans and heading to the door.

##

"Word around campus is that you're dancing at Norma Jeans." Cammie thought that was a bit out of character for her roommate. "What? Who told you that?" Vanessa wondered. "Kids from the lacrosse team were there last night. Said you were great," Cammie added with a laugh.

"Why would I do that? What my scholarship doesn't cover, Mom's professorial benefit does."

"I guess girls do it for lots of reasons." Vanessa thought, she knows me better. Then a thought crossed her mind. She checked the address and hopped on a bus. It was about an hour and a half before she was staring face-to-face with herself, swaying naked on that stage, twisting around the pole, gathering dollars. "I wonder," she thought to herself.

Olya walked right to her table after she left the stage. "Vanessa?" She just stared. "Great to finally meet you. I hoped you would come. Olya," she said, extending her hand for a shake.

"I'm going to kill you." A figure of speech. "I thought you were in Europe."

"A little vacation. I get around."

"I'm planning on getting a security clearance and keeping my scholarship."

"You mean my scholarship?"

Vanessa said nothing, only glared. "I thought this would be a fun way to meet you. Anyhow, today's my last day."

"Sessai will kill you. How did you get here? Do you need money?"

"Don't worry about me. Really, we can try to be sisters. How is Tom, by the way."

"Sisters? Ha..." Vanessa glanced away and back at Olya. "What did you do there? He called me non-stop for two weeks and suggested visiting me here multiple times."

Olya smirked. "This is actually a bit tame compared to what happened at Cornell. I was on a bit of an emotional ride at the time. Cut off from my life, and all."

Vanessa took a deep breath. "Listen, I hear you are well settled in Europe and Sessai tells me you have an awesome future in store. This is the only place where this kind of thing can be a disaster for me."

"Really, I just wanted to meet you. Ok, I wanted to take a dig, since you are enjoying what I worked so hard for. I'm not sure I can trust Sessai, but if all the things he says are true, you're right, things will be great." Olya looked at Vanessa. "Mostly I miss my Mom."

Vanessa glanced up at the next dancer. "Yeah, I guess I understand that. Call me anytime. Let me know if you need anything." Vanessa handed Olya her telephone number on a small scrap of paper. "Please don't write this on any toilet stall walls."

"Thanks, I won't," said Olya, glancing at the number. "We ought to coordinate interactions with Tom."

"I will let you know if he calls again."

"Okay. Good luck with the lacrosse team," Olya added, smiling.

"Bitch," was Vanessa's response. "Nice to meet you too," said Olya. "Yeah, nice to meet you," said Vanessa, as she got up and walked out the door. Halfway back to campus on the bus, her phone vibrated. "Trust you enjoyed the swords and the books." Ah, so those were from her. Interesting, thought Vanessa.

##

Squeak, squeak, tap, tap. Scratch, scratch, tap, squeak. The little brown man was filling the chalk board with numbers and symbols. He had been hard at work filling the board when they walked in. Trudged in, filling some of the hall. Very poorly attended, this class, in spite of it being a very large lecture hall. He ignored them, and in ones and twos, sixteen of them found seats.

There was Joel, in the back of the class, with a few of his lacrosse minions and the really smart frat brother (geeky, skinny, glasses, crappy sense of humor, but undoubtedly a pretty good tutor). Everyone said Joel was going to serve in the air force after graduation, but she wasn't sure how that worked. Hopkins didn't have air force ROTC.

The two Chinese kids. What were their names? One was writing in a notebook, the other on a laptop. A Lenovo, of course.

The smart track team kid from New Hampshire. They said he had a sprinting record at Exeter.

Six kids from India, one from Pakistan. There was one other girl, who wore "soda pop" glasses and studiously wrote every squiggle from the board. Vanessa remembered she was in the chess club.

They watched while the board slowly filled with lines of mathematics and chemistry. "These figures describe a catalytic converter for a jet that doesn't undermine thrust or fuel efficiency." said the man, when he was done scrawling. "I want the mechanical design of the blades that act as a converter, the composition of the coating and the process for performing the coating. You have until next Friday."

Joel's geeky frat brother asked, "Do we have to use J10 fuel?" The rest of the class took a deep breath while the instructor contemplated a response. Everyone knew the last class received mostly F's and a D. "I am tempted to require you to redesign refinery science for this problem, but I am going to give you … a break. So yes, J10 is a requirement." Joel gave his geek a glance. One of the minions kicked the geek's chair. "That will be all."

Army

"Sir, you wanted to see me?" Vanessa asked the Professor of Military science, an Army lieutenant colonel, who was sitting behind his desk in "class b's." He glanced up at her, and back at the pile of papers on his desk. "Have a seat. Let me finish this page." He was marking someone's paper with red marker. He frowned. Shook his head. Flipped it upside down on a pile next to the one he was working on, and glanced back at Vanessa.

"Congratulations! You've been branched Aviation!" The aviation branch was the part of the Army that flew its aircraft. In point of fact, the US Army had more aircraft than the US Air Force did. Just as it had more boats than the Navy.

Vanessa glanced back. Resolute. "Sir. That was my second choice. I wanted Military Police."

"You are throwing away your aeronautics degree. Ridiculous. The Army can't allow that. Nor can I."

"Sir, please." Vanessa replied. "There is plenty of time for aviation later. There is a war going on, and I want to be part of it. Military police is the only place where a girl can be a part of it."

"Military police handle traffic at intersections and military discipline problems. You are committing career suicide."

"No sir. The military police units are getting infantry missions in Iraq. It's the only place in the Army where women are serving right next to men, expected to perform as they do, in life and death situations. That's where I need to be as a lieutenant. Besides, I'm a leader, not a technician. I will be leading a few dozen troops as an MP officer, right away. If I go aviation, I will be driving an aircraft with no leadership responsibility for years."

The lieutenant colonel frowned.

"And I can go to aviation school after my initial tour. Right?" Vanessa asked, hopeful she convinced him.

"Hmm," he said. "So you want to request the Army reverse your branch selection?"

"Yes sir." He nodded. "Okay."

##

"The North Atlantic council has a huge staff, including yours truly, and serves as a forum for plenty of pan-European issues," adding, "not typically much about Ukraine." Olya continued: "Although the United States' European Command, with its four star general, the SACEUR, plays an overbearing role, NATO is run by its civilian council, and all specific military actions are directed by NATO's military committee." Olya glanced at Sessai then Stefan. "Perhaps it isn't rocket science, but that is the run-down. The military committee is chaired by a European general, although the deputy is always an American three-star, typically from the Air Force."

"No, it's helpful." Said Stefan. "How is your Russian?" asked Sessai. "Horosho," answered Olya, then she described some details about her immediate NATO management and some important dynamics associated with the sitting military committee members… in Russian. Sessai and Stefan exchanged glances. "We think you are ready to go to Belorussia." Said Stefan.

"Those guys are still communist. How can you send me there? Anyway, I'm still getting adjusted to this NATO thing."

Stefan answered: "It's an administrative exchange with Ukraine. Sessai and I have been sending great people there for six or so years… we met the president of the country before he was elected to that office, and the rotation is scheduled for two months from today. No problem."

Sessai added: "It's time for you to say good bye to that pilot fellow anyhow." Olya looked at him. How did he know about that, she wondered. She paused. "So its settled?" Asked Stefan. "It's a third world country," she answered, her last feeble attempt to argue. "Living like royalty in a third world country isn't a bad deal," answered Stefan, considering the plan final. "This time we will handle everything, apartment, bank account… maybe even boyfriend," added Sessai with a smirk.

"Okay," she answered.

##

"Sir. Lieutenant Smith reports." Captain Roman glanced up from the stack of papers on his desk. Fort Bragg had no end of paperwork for a Military Police company commander. Blotter reports for many of the units on the base. Enlisted Evaluation Reports to review and send back. Officer Evaluation reports to write and re-write after Adjutant and Battalion Commander edits.

Roman leaned back in his chair and returned with a sloppy salute. "Have a seat." Nodded his head, taking her in. "Pretty girl," he thought. "Welcome to Bravo company," he said.

"Thank you sir," she replied, taking a seat.

"So… usually I'd be appointing you to be my operations officer. Basically assisting the operations sergeant with training schedules and improving lesson plans from the company. Great experience for a future platoon leader, and a great way to get to know the battalion lay of the land." Roman paused. His new second lieutenant was silent. Expressionless. "There are three other lieutenants waiting for a platoon. One of them is doing a pretty good job in the Operations role. I'm leaving him there. The other two are fuck-ups," he continued. "Off the record."

"Yes sir," she replied. He went on. "You are in luck. Judy Collier just lodged a sexual harassment complaint about the battalion commander. So she's out. And you… are in."

Vanessa's eyes went wide. "It's all a bit complicated, but the Adjutant and Brigade staff thought the best thing for my company and your new platoon would be if Judy steps down effective today and for various…" he glanced at her again, biting his lip, "political reasons, we need to put a woman in the job."

Vanessa inhaled. "Am I ready for this?" she wondered. "So you are making me a platoon leader?" Vanessa asked. "Yes I am," he answered.

He was silent. "She is going to screw this up totally," he thought. It's a disservice to her, the platoon and the company. There is no way she is ready.

"I hear you know how to handle a blade." It was a statement. They had heard about the fencing team. "Yes sir," she answered. "Well, that won't help much in Iraq. But at least you're in shape."

He paused, assessing how she was taking the news. "There are three relief for cause NCOER's that need to be completed: get them from the Adjutant. Then get out to the range and make sure everyone does clearing procedures on those M2's. I also want you to draw your new rifle today and get it cleaned. Understood?"

Vanessa had pulled a small notebook from her pocket and was furiously scribbling. "Yes sir," she answered. "Your platoon sergeant's name is Fred Swahili. Sergeant First Class Swahili. You will find him in the platoon office. Second platoon. Stay out of his way." She glanced at Captain Roman.

"Yes sir." He wrapped things up: "We depart for Iraq in three months. I expect the platoon to be ready."

Roman pursed his lips. "Any questions?" he asked her. "No sir." Then she stood, saluted, and left his office.

She walked into the beige building with the "Second Platoon" sign over the door. Walked into the platoon office, where a woman was putting some things in a box. The woman, a brunette, turned to look at Vanessa. She was wearing black, first lieutenant bars. Her name tape, under the airborne and air assault wings, said "Collier." The woman frowned and said, "I don't need any help packing."

Vanessa backed out of the doorway, but into the office. "Okay," Vanessa answered, quickly understanding Judy Collier assumed the second lieutenant standing in her office had been sent from battalion or brigade to expedite the departure. Vanessa watched Lieutenant Collier walk out with her box, muttering "over a year, and this is the treatment I get."

Vanessa watched her walking for a few seconds then turned to the middle aged black man sitting behind the desk. "Sergeant Swahili?"

"Yes," he answered, grimly. "I'm Vanessa Smith. Captain Roman just made me second platoon leader."

Swahili looked at her. His cheeks filled with air. Son of a bitch, he thought, subtly shaking his head. "How many NCOERs are in the works?" Vanessa asked him.

Swahili put both his hands on his face, rubbing it. Then he glanced up at her and opened his top drawer. From there he took a notebook and opened it, replying, "Five. Three relief for cause and two annuals."

"Okay. I will go collect the drafts from the Adjutant. When I get back, I'd like to visit the machine gun range. Can you have my driver meet me in the motor pool?"

"Specialist Kaverian is already in the motor pool. He is working on Lieutenant Collier's.. umm.. your …

hummer." Swahili thought for a second. "The Adjutant only has the three relief for cause NCOERs. I'm still working on the two annuals." He glanced at her again. "Come to think of it, I think Gonzalez's change of rater is due back. Get that one too."

"Okay," she answered him. "Does Kaverian know how to get to the range or do I need to get a map?"

"A map," Swahili scoffed. "Just what I need to do is give a second lieutenant a map." He glanced at her again, with a bit of a frown. "Kaverian knows how to get there. Don't forget to wear your LCE."

"I won't," Vanessa replied. "Sorry about everything," she said, as she left for the NCOERs. "Certainly not your fault," she heard the old man say, but she kept walking. She didn't see the rapid walk that SFC Swahili made to Captain Roman's office and she certainly would not have appreciated hearing the conversation that ensued there, nor the one between Swahili and the first sergeant that happened shortly thereafter. Everyone had thoughts about who the new platoon leader should be. She wasn't him.

Battalion headquarters were a short walk away. Vanessa poked her head in the door with the "S3 Operations" sign above it. There was a second lieutenant, a first lieutenant and an overweight female master sergeant sitting at three of the four desks. The fourth desk was empty, with the name "Captain Roland M. Fossier" at the front. There was a small blue flag, or guidon, with "A Company" embroidered on it, framed on the wall behind Fossier's desk.

"Excuse me," Vanessa asked, "Can you tell me which fifty cal range Bravo second platoon is using today?" The first lieutenant said, "Sure" and grabbed a clip board. After glancing at it, he replied "They are on Audie Murphy. South side."

"Is there some place I can get a map?" she asked him. The second lieutenant chimed in: "You can have this one." He offered her a map, which she took. She glanced at it, and found "Audie Murphy" among the hashed colored shapes on the map. "Do you need it back?" She asked him.

"No. That's okay. I can get another." he scraped his bottom lip with his top teeth. "New bravo ops officer?" Vanessa took the map, quietly saying "thanks" and nodding her head. Then she replied, "no, new platoon leader," as she turned and retreated toward the Adjutant's office.

"Shit," she thought to herself. So unladylike. "One of those lieutenants probably thought he was getting my platoon…"

##

"Here Ma'am. Secure this holster on your LCE somewhere. Can't be on the range without at least appearing armed." Kavarian smiled as he handed her the holster. "Thanks," she said, climbing in. "You know how to get there?" She asked.

"Pretty much," he said. He pulled out of the motor pool and headed the direction of the ranges. Vanessa pulled out her new map. "Where'd you get that?" Kavarian asked. "S3," she answered, sorting through which little black square was passing on the right. "Do you qualify on the M2?" she wondered.

"Sure. Sarge says everyone needs to be able to jump up behind one. Like Audie Murphy." Vanessa smiled. "Right. Just like Audie Murphy. Do you think Sarge is already on the range?"

"I imagine so," her driver said. "He likes to make sure things are squared away."

When they arrived, Vanessa found SFC Swahili. "How are things?" she asked. "Fine," he answered, without a glance. "Okay. I'm going to head back in to clean my M4. Can you have everyone shout clearing procedures when they get back to the barracks?"

"They aren't children, Ma'am," he said. "Have we had any accidental discharges this year?" she asked.

He bit his lip. "You will hear us," he replied. She jumped back in next to Kavarian and handed him the holster. "Arms room," she said. "Roger," he replied, without fanfare.

Barbarella, the armorer, was a bit surprised to see her. "I don't have your weapons card prepared, sorry Ma'am." She wondered if he couldn't just have her sign a hand receipt. Instead, he completed the card with a pen and had her sign it. "Thanks," she answered, pulling the charging handle to the rear immediately after receiving the rifle. "I should be done around 5. Will you be here?"

"I'm working off gigs. Will be here until at least 6."

"Great. See you in a few hours."

##

"First I remove the magazine, then pull the charging handle to the rear, Sergeant," Vanessa heard someone yell. "Then I release the bolt, then I pull the trigger and place the weapon on safe, Sergeant." She heard those words repeated multiple times. Different voices, although an occasional repeat.

After it stopped, Sergeant Swahili appeared in the office. She glanced up, but quickly returning her attention on a few final swipes. He noticed the NCOERs on his desk. "Thanks," he said.

She glanced over. "If you want, I can take a look at those annuals. I'm headed to the Arms room to turn this in." He nodded.

##

Two Hummers pulled in to the gate, M2's facing the sky, clear of rounds. Soldiers jumped out, removing magazines, pulling charging handles to the rear, releasing bolts and pulling triggers. Vanessa was the last in line. "Bad news, ma'am" said the sergeant of the guard. "Sergeant Bonfiglio's patrol failed inspection." She glanced at him. "What's the route?" she asked. "Two blocks east of yours, a bit further south." She glanced at her patrol. "When was the last time we ran that route?" she asked. "According to S2, three days ago."

"Okay, Soldiers, gather 'round. We're going out again," Vanessa called. "You have to be shitting me!" hollered Rodriguez. Sanders sniped, "Hey, you didn't want to see the Dallas Cowboy Cheerleaders any how…" Another said, "Aw, man, Ally Trainer so has a crush on me." Amanda Han scowled. Vanessa glanced at Amanda and smiled: "Hey guys, I'm more heartbroken than any of you."

She showed them the route. Had everyone change passcode and frequencies. They mounted the hummers, pulled up to the circle, around it and back to exit the gate. "Locked and loaded," she called. "Locked and loaded," was the unison answer, as everyone's weapons clacked.

Five hundred meters down the road Rodriguez shouted "activity on the right." Vanessa's gunner said, "yeah, I see it" but there was a large flash and a ferocious explosion. Vanessa was thrown from the vehicle. When her ears stopped ringing, she glanced around. Her vehicle was upside down. The other was on its side, burning. Her M4 was ten feet away, but appeared functional.

She grabbed it, glancing where Rodriguez had suggested. A skinny dark haired man ran out of a doorway, then stopped when he saw Vanessa. She shouldered her rifle, and as he started to turn, she squeezed off three rounds. The man dropped.

When she looked at her vehicles, she saw no movement. There was some blood. She ran to one vehicle… just goo and broken bodies. In the distance, she heard motors. "The QRF," she thought, running to the next vehicle. The gunner was crushed under the vehicle, everyone else had been shredded with shrapnel.

Vanessa glanced at her uniform, realizing it was also shredded.

The QRF grew closer, and Vanessa grabbed her backpack. She stepped into a building and pulled her toilet paper from the bag. "I shouldn't have survived this," she muttered to herself. "What to do."

##

"We're sending you to work for General Redgrave," Captain Roman had said. "Best thing for the platoon is for us to roll everyone into the other units." She hadn't argued. "You are lucky to be alive," he had said. Sometimes it didn't feel that way, but it was true. General Redgrave was the highest ranking woman in Iraq at the time. When she reported for duty, the General had asked, "What are you going to do now?"

Everything had happened so fast. There was a medal. A few formations, where people talked about her valor. And about how lucky she was to be alive.

"Flight school," Vanessa had said. "My ROTC leadership suggested I go aviation in the first place. But I wanted combat leadership experience." The general had been silent for a moment. "Well, I'd say you made the right decision, but frankly, you shouldn't be alive." Redgrave studied her. "I have examined all the reports. There was nothing you could have done, short of canceling the patrol. Taking out the trigger man, incredible shooting. Just take it easy. Of course, I've heard you are a "cool hand Luke," but some people lose perspective upon promotion to captain."

"Yes, I know," Vanessa had replied. Being an aide was a busy experience, which helped her keep her mind off the men and woman that she lost. She was glad when her tour ended, and she climbed an airplane for Bragg. Redgrave had been a great boss.

##

Day three formation at Fort Rucker. Vanessa had gotten up early, as usual, and went for a run. The wind and warm sun were exhilarating. The announcement came as a surprise. And brought back a memory: "If you wait until your commitment is complete, you may stay as long as you want." Sessai had said. Suddenly Vanessa was very curious. And less interested in becoming a pilot.

The announcement: "Candidates. There is a draw-down coming. If any of you wish to leave the service, you may resign. All previous commitments are negated. Of course, if you complete pilot training, you will incur a new obligation and will be required to stay."

To the shock of her colleagues, Vanessa put her hand up. The staff tried to talk her out of it. Major Roman called to tell her it was normal to be disgusted after losing a team, but reminding her that the Army had a wonderful future in store for her.

General Redgrave even called. Vanessa simply shared that she had a family commitment, that she had to go to Japan. "I have been authorized to offer you a 90 day leave, to consider your options. In three months, you can return to the Army and resume your aviation training. We want to keep you, Vanessa."

"Thank you, Ma'am. Thanks for everything." Vanessa replied. She packed her uniforms and small collection of furniture in a storage unit, then went to the airport.

##

"Tom, there is a blonde here to see you. Says her name is Vanessa Smith, that she knew you some years ago," the beautiful brunette glanced up at Vanessa. "He will be right down," Sandy told her. "Hand me your ID."

Vanessa passed her a driver's license and received a white "visitors badge" in return. In a moment, Tom walked into the lobby and gave her a big hug. "Wow, I didn't think I'd ever see you again," he said.

"Me too," she replied. "It's good to see you."

"Well, it isn't much, but let's chat in my office." She followed him through the halls, up a staircase and into a small room with windows and two desks.

"So.. a hero!" Tom had said. She brushed it aside. "And here you are, crushing it in Silicon Valley!" was her answer.

"Ha. Fifty percent of these people are smarter than me. The other fifty percent have better experience for what we're doing." Tom said with a smile, then more seriously, "Hey, I'm sorry about being so... angry."

Vanessa thought about the angry emails. The couple angry messages. "It's okay. I guess I'd have been very upset too. Hard to believe I didn't remember anything, I guess."

"Well," he felt he had to respond. "Too much testosterone. We all grow up, eventually." He smiled.

"Funny thing is, I still don't. But I'm curious… about the girl you knew."

"You?"

"Are you sure it was me?" Ha, he laughed. "Well, except for that brief, crazy visit at Cornell, you didn't let me get close after we broke up, so it's hard to say, I guess. But you sure looked the same. Voice sounded the same."

"Mannerisms the same? Exactly the same?"

"What are you thinking, some kind of Salt thing," he said, referring to an Angelina Jolie movie they had seen on an early date, where Soviet agents were planted across the USA. "Ah, that's right, you don't remember."

She had seen the movie. "Nothing like that. It's just strange. I was highly functional at Hopkins, and in the Army. But I have absolutely no memories of early childhood or.. or even any of my parents."

"That is .. a bit odd. I guess. What did the doctors say?"

"Usually most memory comes back. Or at least some. But there wasn't, and even isn't, a shred of memory about Mom and Dad."

"How are Bill and Julie?" He asked. "Great," she answered. "How are yours?"

"Good." He shrugged. "And now?"

"I can leave the Army or stay. If I stay, I'll learn to fly helicopters. Unsure about what I'll do if I leave. Spending a few months in Japan, starting tomorrow."

"We'd hire you in a second."

"Ha, ha. With my outdated aeronautics degree?"

"In a second, girl. What's in Japan"

She smiled. "Thanks. We'll see. An old friend of the family lives in Japan. Maybe we can chat some more on email. It's good to see you."

"Likewise," he said. She gave him a big hug and kiss at the door, after returning her badge and claiming her license. "I love you," she said, a bit too loud.

"Good luck with that receptionist," she texted from the car.

"Bitch," was his reply. "She has a master's in Art History, BTW." She smiled. And pointed her car to the San Francisco airport.

Japan

Sessai was delighted to see her. "Perhaps you are wondering what a Buddhist monk from India was doing in Warsaw after World War II, at a YMCA? My story, and I guess yours, began in India five hundred years before Christ."

I was born there a wealthy boy, but not a first born one, and so my parents gave me to Siddhartha to learn the ways of Buddhism and to help his order.

I saw, after a bit, that some of the monks were better preserved than others. And the wisdom they shared.. well.. seemed beyond the years of one man. Of course, many monks say they have lived previous lives, but in fact, they have lived for longer than one lifetime.

This reality isn't something a normal boy can learn in ten years, but I suppose I wasn't a normal boy. I paid more attention than most. I went to Siddhartha at ten, and began to work with one of his disciples. That disciple taught me the reflections of a monk, but also the training of a body guard, because, of course, Siddhartha was a Brahmin, no ordinary Indian man, and some of us (in those days) were needed to protect the order.

Since my family were big, and strong, of course I was selected to be among the protectors. My disciple was also a big and strong man, and, at the time I met him, a man of two lifetimes. He built my strength and also my training with spear and sword. Some might say it is strange for a monk to learn such things, but my disciple knew them and he taught them to me.

In my twentieth year, I made a rather big scene, because my disciple had taught me many things, which he had learned in life, and because of how he taught me, I knew he experienced them. How does a man live to be more than a hundred years old?

I got in an argument with one of the other men, about our disciple, and that he had lived longer than most. I was telling him that I was also going to live beyond a hundred years, because I was a better student of the spear and sword art. The other student only said it wasn't so, and I was giving him a thrashing with a staff when our disciple stopped me, easily removing staff from my hands and throwing me across the room.

How was it possible for such a little man to throw me so far, I had wondered. And when he pinned me to the ground, to quell my rage, I knew there was something else unusual about him. He was, by far, stronger than I, and also seemed to possess the weight of the moon in him.

I struggled until I was tired, which was quite a long time, gazing into his peaceful face, until finally he said I must stop struggling and listen. He said I must never talk again about living more than a hundred years, and if I make such a promise, that he will tell me more about it.

"Of course I promise," I had said. And once I did, he let me up. "Later," he suggested, before walking away. Later, it turned out, was in my twenty fifth year. He made me wait five years to hear the secret and to begin induction. I won't make you wait five years to hear the secret, but you must also promise not to tell it, Vanessa, at least not to anyone who won't join our order.

"Do you promise?" he asked her. "Who would I tell," she asked. He gazed at her pretty face, so serious. So apparently young. "You still don't remember anything, do you?" He asked.

"I remember college, and the Army. Both of those, quite well. But the things before, no, I don't. They said that's pretty unusual at this stage." She said. "You will," he replied. "Perhaps after you meet your father. Or perhaps later today. It's hard to tell.

This isn't unusual, this memory loss.. well, that unusual. After a sleeping."

They woke me after two hundred years, of my first sleeping. They woke me and told me I had to go to Egypt. Somehow I knew the Egyptian language, and I didn't know how. I had learned it before going into that first long sleep, much as I taught you English before your last sleeping, but I hadn't remembered that. Until later.

"You taught me English?" she asked. "Yes," he replied. "I taught you in 1948, in New York City. You don't remember that, yet, but you will remember those days. You also know Ukrainian and Russian." Then he switched into another tongue, and somehow she understood him.

They gave me instructions regarding how to get to Egypt and also that there were arts there, that they discovered, about sleeping, that I needed to learn. They told me who I needed to find in Egypt and how to find him. They didn't tell me that I knew Egyptian, although I learned I knew it when I arrived there, after crossing many lands where I didn't understand a word. Suddenly, I understood.

Sessai looked at her, and a smile crept across his face. "You are handling this well, this mystery." She stared at him. "You taught me English, in New York City, in 1948? That is ridiculous."

"Perhaps in the world you think you live in. But not in the one that you and I inhabit."

When I arrived in Egypt, they were preparing two people for a sleeping, a man and a woman. The man's name was Antony. I only learned the woman's name later. I helped seal the boxes. They told me about the process leading to the boxing, and about the sleeping. They also told me that I would be taking her box to Europe, where ever that was, which is why I had to learn Ukrainian.

It was a bit strange that I should go to Europe over land, because boat would have been much easier, and avoided so much conflict. But people were worried that someone might break open the box, if we went by ship, so I left in the night, for Damascus. I traveled to Pilate, who promised to watch the box for me, for a time, and asked me to protect a Man for a bit.

I told Pilate I had been instructed to go to Ukraine, although they didn't call it that in those days. He had smiled and assured me there was no rush, and that he would keep her safe. He also taught me a few words of Hebrew, but promised my Egyptian would suit me fine for his purposes. "You just have to keep this Yeshua safe," he said before introducing me to Judas.

"Yeshua. You met Yeshua?" Vanessa asked. "Yes. Do you really think James cut that man's ear off?" She thought for a moment. "No, I guess not." He went on: "In any event, Yeshua told me not to fight, so I let them take Him. After that fiasco, I went to Pilate, collected her box and resumed the trip to Europe. I brought her to the caves in Kiev, and told people there that she was an Egyptian mummy and that they should leave her alone. It transpired that people remembered my lie about the mummy part but forgot the instructions that she be left alone. In 1700, when they broke into her box, people thought ground mummy had magical and medicinal powers.

"What a mistake," he said solemnly. "Why are you telling me this? I don't care about all these legends and… farfetched tales. I want to hear about me. About why I am so strong. About this order that you keep telling me about. And as for the Ukrainian father you mentioned earlier, I know my parents and they both live in Kansas. They taught me English, when I was a little girl." Vanessa was annoyed.

"Do you remember learning English from them as a little girl? Do you remember being a little girl?" He asked her. "No one remembers being a little girl," Vanessa replied. "Besides, there was an accident." He gazed at her. "Yes, there was an accident, but not the one you are thinking about. Your accident happened in Warsaw and it was because of Cleo."

"Cleo?" She hadn't heard that name before. At least.. she didn't remember hearing that name, in any context related to her own. "Yes," answered Sessai. The first time I actually saw her was shortly after I met your father. Although I had known about her for already a thousand years.

After I deposited that box in the Kievan caves, I was essentially a free man. I pondered returning to India and perhaps finding a monastery there. Instead I stayed in the Caves in Kiev, meeting the local Scoloti, tending sheep and fashioning a life of sorts. After I had been there some decades, watching the Romans come and go, I saw Commodus' success against the lazyges, and decided I needed a quality blade. Assuming Cleo was safely at rest, I began my search for a perfect sword.

"And why is this Cleo important?" Sessai looked at her, assessing. Was it time to tell Vanessa this truth? He decided that it was.

Sessai continued, "I met your father in 1705. We had heard some rumors about a vampire sighting, or at least two bloody killings. Usually these rumors were someone trying to evade blame, but when I exhumed the bodies, the damage to ribs and skull was.." he glanced at Vanessa, "remarkable."

Sessai continued: "There had been a big victory celebration, and I thought, logically, that she might have gone there. Who knew what she would be up to, or what the state of her memory might be. Within an hour of her awakening, she already had two kills, so I was concerned."

"People were talking about the marriages, and about the champion of East Bank." Sessai glanced at Vanessa. "So it happened, your father was the champion of East Bank. He had chosen Cleo to be his wife, but she was not around. All the other young champions had brides, but the one, the foremost, your father, he was alone. Then I saw the marks on his neck."

"Marks?" Vanessa asked. "Yes, marks," replied Sessai. "I asked your father how he came to acquire them, and he evaded answering. He was embarrassed. I am certain the situation, to be abandoned by his wife, was quite embarrassing for him. But eventually he admitted where he got them. And after spending some time with him, observing and questioning, I realized he would have to be inducted."

"Inducted?" asked Vanessa.

Sessai turned away, philosophical. Took a deep breath and gazed back at her. "Vanessa, I know I told you, at Hopkins, that when you came to me, you would be able to stay for as long as you want. You have waited a long time to hear the truth. But I think its best you hear it from your father. I think it's best you go to Ukraine."

##

After Vanessa stomped off, Sessai walked into the kitchen to pour himself a cup of tea. What self-respecting samurai would have a samovar to make his tea? One, thought Sessai. Then he thought about the circumstances leading to that samovar.

He and Stefan had made the trip to Brest with such excitement. At last, it seemed an opportunity for Kievan democracy. Stefan had unearthed Mazeppa's sword, carefully wrapped and boxed it (with several bottles of fine Ukraine vodka), certain that they would find Myechyslaw Hryb, Chairman of Belorus, and convince him to unify the two countries in honor of the great Kievan Rus empire. Instead, they and their vodka had been hijacked by an oaf named Lukashenko, who ogled the sword and regaled them with stories of his hockey prowess. When Lukashenko was elected president of

Belarus several years later, Sessai and Stefan congratulated themselves on parting with those bottles of vodka.

"Perhaps it is time to revisit our old friend," thought Sessai.

##

Vanessa was very surprised to understand the language when she walked off the airplane in Kiev, Ukraine. Most people tried broken, heavily accented English ("Taxi?" they asked. "Foreign exchange?"). She walked to the cash machine, with it's marked "anti-fraud" instructions, and withdrew 10,000 hrevnia. Then, walking to the door, she began studying her options.

Tall and short men. Black hair and blonde. Skinny and chunky. There were no women. Just outside the door, a fellow was talking to a friend. The friend was smoking.

"How much to the center of Kiev," she asked him in Russian. "200 HUA," was his curt reply. "Too much," she responded. He shrugged. "Do you have a map of the city?" When he answered, "yes," she said okay, and followed him to his cab.

Small talk. Not really her thing, but perhaps she might learn something. So she and the taxi driver chatted pleasantly about parents, children, weather, American college and contrasts with Ukraine college, which the man had attended. He dropped her off at Saint Michaels, with her small bag. After she checked the bag and the coat, she asked the coat check lady, "How might I find Stefan Cossack. I was told his was the best tour."

"Is he expecting you?" the woman asked. "His tour started thirty minutes ago. You have already missed the best part." Vanessa smiled. "It's alright. Can you take me to him?"

The woman frowned. "Well, I suppose. There isn't anyone here and the courtyard is empty. Right this way." She scurried up the small staircase and across the room. Vanessa glanced around the room with interest, but kept closely to the woman's heels. They climbed another staircase, this one more narrow, around a bend, and into the air. There was a crowd of people and a man, athletic, not young, not old, talking with his back to her. The woman gestured to her, than scurried back down the staircase.

Vanessa quietly stepped behind the crowd and listened. Stefan was talking with animation about the bells, about how they had been restored. "Excuse me," Vanessa interrupted, "is this restoration accurate to the bells that Mazeppa had originally installed?"

Stefan looked at her and his mouth dropped open. Tears welled up in his eyes. "Olya" he said quietly, smiling. He glanced at the crowd, and said "Excuse me for a moment." (Prostite mney). He took the five steps toward Vanessa and gave her a big bear hug. She hugged him back. "it's so good to see you," he said. She didn't remember him.

Later, on his balcony, after borscht and vegetables, sipping coffee, Stefan told Vanessa about her real mother. Golden blonde hair. As sweet and devoted as a landed princess might be.

Vanessa had told Stefan what Sessai had told her to say: "We have found your mother. She is alive." Stefan had been taken aback. Breathing several deep breaths.. and looking back at her. "No," he had replied. "Your mother has been dead for two hundred years. Sessai meant" adding ominously, "he has found Cleo. Or at least thinks he has."

"When I awoke from my first sleeping, I wasn't able to remember anything either. There must have been a loud clicking sound, and the box lid swung open. I opened my eyes… pitch black… I felt the steel next to me… instinctively grabbing it and hoisting myself from the box. I stumbled around that small cave for some minutes, pushing against the wall. Finally, the wall moved."

I walked into the sunlight and looked around. It was early spring time. Birds were singing… such a beautiful sight. I remember glancing back into the cave, trying to remember why I was there and marveling at the size of the rock that I had just displaced. I saw a road in the distance and walked to it. After getting there, I followed some wagon tracks east.

There was a town a few miles from there… I arrived mid-day and asked for a blacksmith, thinking I would be able to get work. The blacksmith took one look at the steel, Mazeppa's sword, and grabbed my sleeve: "Where did you get this?" he had asked.

I didn't know what to say, so I just shrugged. He dragged me to a nearby inn, where I met your grandfather for the first time. The blacksmith pushed me in front of your grandfather, and said "Gospodin, we have a visitor."

The man glanced at me and shrugged. "So?" He asked, almost laughing. The blacksmith handed him Mazeppa's sword, at which point your grandfather stopped laughing. "Where did you get this?" he asked.

"My family," I responded, uncertain what else to say. "Where are you from, man?" The farmer asked. Again, unsure what to say, I responded, "the West."

"The West," repeated the farmer, who glanced at the blacksmith. "You need a job?" he asked me. "Yes, Gospodin," I had responded. "And some food." I realized suddenly that I was incredibly hungry. The farmer pushed his plate to me, then told me I would work on his farm, that he needed help, and that he would watch the sword until it was time for me to move on.

The farmer, your grandfather, glanced at the blacksmith, then said, "Work on the farm is hard, but it's the best place on the East Bank. I need a foreman. If you have come by this sword honestly, I will be able to tell quickly."

I wasn't paying much attention, though I probably should have been. A two hundred year sleeping makes a man hungry. Very hungry. They could see I was hungry and let me eat. Then the farmer took me to the homestead, a place that would be my home for the next fifteen years.

"When did you meet my mother," Vanessa asked. "A few days later," Stefan replied. There was a dance, kind of a folk gathering. Your grandfather used to do them quite regularly in those days. Really, the high point of the month for everyone in the village. At one point, a couple of the other farm workers started doing the Cossack dance. One of the other workers told me to try it. I didn't know it at the time, but my legs remembered. I was quite good at that dance. So they christened me "Cossack"… Stefan Cossack. And it impressed your mother, that dance.

That was when I first saw her, watching me dance, laughing with the other girls. She was radiant, a beauty. Someone whispered that she was the farmer's daughter. I decided then and there that I would marry her. And I did… but it was many years later… impressing your grandfather was not easy.

"How long was it, after your waking, before you remembered?" Vanessa asked.

Stefan was silent. Thoughtful. "Several weeks," he answered. "They took me to work on the southern fields. The aroma of the flowers, the gurgling brook. The grain, already above my head, swaying in the wind." He smiled. "A Cossack's heart and mind are tightly bound to his land." Stefan took Vanessa's hand. "Tomorrow we will take you there. Perhaps it will have the same effect on you that it had on me."

"Sessai mentioned you were married to Cleo. But she is not my mother?" Vanessa needed clarification.

"Yes," answered Stefan, rubbing his chin. "There was a ceremony. Quite an embarrassment, actually. After we unified East and West banks, there was a huge celebration. It was there that I first saw Cleo. She was hanging around the edges. No one knew who she was. She had softly whispered, "So you are the champion of the East Bank?" at one point in the celebration, and I grabbed her to kiss her.

Stefan glanced at his daughter. "My actions that day were not gentlemanly, but please understand they were common for the day. I was the champion of East Bank and of course assumed that Cleo would be delighted to have this gift from me."

"And so you were married?" Vanessa asked. Laughing sadly, Stefan responded, "no, Cleo avoided my kiss, rolled away and swiftly walked into the crowd, wagging her finger at me as she did. But later that evening, when Mazeppa asked what brides and grooms would be presented, I saw her and called her out."

"I don't understand," Vanessa was puzzled.

"We had spent months, some of us years, in the saddle, with Mazeppa. We would continue our service, of course, and it was tradition at times like this to declare marriages. I declared Cleo was mine. There was a hasty ceremony, for she, for me, and a dozen other couples. Cleo had made it clear it wasn't what she wanted, but she had no status, and I was hotly pursuing her."

"So she was your wife?" Vanessa asked, indignant.

Stefan gazed over their dinner table, out from the balcony, out over the church, to the crowds and the fairgrounds in the distance and around at the scenery. He turned to look at his daughter. "She could have avoided the marriage ceremony, of course, given who she was, but didn't. She walked demurely at my side, even walked into our bed chamber later that evening. But when I tried to take her," Stefan said, with a sideways glance, "she gripped my hands and rolled me onto my back. Frankly I was shocked. Never had I met a person so strong and certainly not seen such strength in a woman."

Vanessa glanced back intently.

"She had a smile on her lips when she asked me if I had expected to be bested that evening. Such a question might have been a playful exchange between lovers, but Cleo wasn't playing. She ravaged my neck and I slipped into a sleepy fog. The next day, as we were celebrating, I met Sessai for the first time."

"He told me about meeting you, and spending some time with you after the biting."

Yes, and eventually Sessai asked to join our cavalry. So I introduced him to Mazeppa. Sessai would occasionally slip away, searching for Cleo, he would say, but always he would return, and always frustrated. And so he was by my side, and Mazeppa's, at Poltava, where Ukraine was dealt a terrible disaster.

"So strictly speaking," Stefan finally answered his daughter, "she wasn't my wife, because we never consummated our relationship. Sessai made a point of that… during the induction. He told me this monster, Cleo, was a monster of historic proportions, and that I would be advised to keep my spiritual distance. Of course, she gave me the order, but a marriage would have been too much."

Stefan frowned. "Sessai was right about that." Vanessa asked, "The order?" Her father answered, "The virus. The biting. She gave it to me. And thru some strange miracle, or disaster, I'm not sure which, I passed it to you."

He continued. "It was after Poltava that Sessai saw her for the first time. He said he had escorted her box many years before, but he had no idea what she looked like, since the box was sealed. From a hilltop, with a telescope, I pointed her out to him. That was right before my first sleeping. After he put me in a box, Sessai later told me, he went to find Cleo."

"What a story," she said after a pause. "It's late," Stefan replied, smiling: "Let's do the normal human thing, and get some sleep."

##

In the morning, they found his small green car in the street and drove south. They talked more, along the way.

Finally, they arrived. So many little huts. Neat, orderly rows of crops, patches within hairlines of trees. They left the car near one hut and walked down a path. The summer breeze brushed Vanessa's cheek. Flowers, perhaps like the ones her father had mentioned earlier, added a sweet joyful smell to the wind. As they rounded the ridge of trees and were able to see across the field of wheat, to more trees and a dark navy river threading through the lands in the distance, Vanessa remembered.

She remembered everything.

Remembering

She remembered the summer breeze caught her hair that morning, and brushed it across her cheek. She remembered Holodimir. Warsaw. The freighter to New York with Sessai. Vanessa turned to her father. "Wow." she said.

"Beautiful, yes?" he asked her. "Yes, but… in a flash, I have remembered. So many … terrible… beautiful… memories."

"Yes," he said. "Welcome back."

"But I still have questions," she said. "First, which do you prefer calling me? Olya, Vanessa or Princess?" She smiled, eyes sparkling. "If you answer when I call you, I don't care which!" her father answered. "Of course, your mother named you Olga, or Olya… so, there are some points for that name."

"What happens now?" Vanessa asked. "I joined the American military. I can go back. But I want to stay with you, here."

"Can you stay?" he asked. "Yes. A rather long story, but yes, I can," Vanessa replied.

"After your awakening, Sessai came to see me. He had seen you at the American University. He said you were studying aeronautics. Have you continued that study?"

"Yes, I received a bachelor's of science in aeronautics," Vanessa replied.

"Were you a pilot in the American Army?" Vanessa smiled. "No, but if I go back, I will become one." He glanced at her. "Jets?" he asked.

Vanessa laughed. "No. Helicopters." Stefan worked the lock on the hut they approached. The door opened. Inside, a medium sized space with two large enclosed chairs. "Simulators," thought Vanessa. Stefan looked at her and walked to a bookshelf. On it were notebooks, with labels. "A10 Avionics." "F16 Weapon Systems." etc. "Why not jets?" Stefan asked.

"For the most part, the American Army doesn't have jets. Those are in the Navy and Air Force. And the Marines, in the event you consider that a separate service. The Americans consider the Marines a part of the Navy." A gratuitous point from an Army captain.

Stefan responded: "We have gone through some lengths to acquire these. Sophisticated training machines for the American A10 air to ground combat system and the F16 multi-purpose aircraft. Simulators."

"Why?" Vanessa wondered. "Ukraine needs your help," Stefan responded. "But we can come back here tomorrow. First, let us enjoy this wonderful day and get reacquainted…." They left the simulators and locked the door to the hut.

##

Sessai collected the box at baggage claim and walked past the cab drivers. "Zdrast," said Stefan as they exchanged hugs, while Vanessa put the box in the back of the van. Vanessa let her father's friend sit in the front seat (they had much to discuss) but Sessai turned to her immediately upon entry.

"How have you enjoyed your return to home?" he asked, smiling.

"I remember everything. Everything except the time with Bill and Julie."

"Wonderful news."

Stefan interjected. "She has also made incredible progress with the simulators. Opted to focus on the A-10's. We believe she is ready to fly the real things."

"But I'm curious Sessai. In Japan you told me a bit about your time with Papa. You told me about Cleo. But there are gaps in your story. Where were you after you left Cleo in Kiev? Why did you leave Ukraine then?" Vanessa pondered the thousand year gap in Sessai's story.

"I think I mentioned Commodus and my search for the perfect blade," responded Sessai.

"Maybe, but it doesn't excuse your neglect of Cleo's box."

"In those days I wandered around with an eye patch and floppy hat. The Goth kings made broad use of iron, but interspersed there would be a "wonder blade," something that we know today was steel, but how such blades were produced, where they came from, was always a mystery."

Sessai continued. "Of course the Romans were the most successful army of the day. I managed to join the Roman Army after being satisfied no one was going to disturb Cleo. I was there when Galerius defeated the

Persians. But I had been thinking about Cleo, about what I had learned about sleeping, and began thinking about finding a secluded spot."

"Unlike yours truly," Stefan interjected, "Sessai had no coach."

"No, that's right. I had been sent to learn a few things from the Egyptians. The monks in India told me about the dangers associated with Cleo. I also had seen how secure her box had been, but there had been hints of significant benefits to sleeping. So I parted ways with the Romans after fighting a few battles with them and traveled north, and somewhat east, to a place the Romans called Gaul. I found a village, with a little shrine there, where a saints remains were supposedly buried. I studied this little shrine for a while, it's little basement, and found a lock that I might put on the basement door."

"I brought my own little comfortable box into that basement. Contemplated the supply of powder that I had. I ingested the powder with some wine, and closed my box over my head. The next thing I knew, someone had opened it. When I opened my eyes, there were four men staring at me."

"I was startled. They were startled. I don't think they were aware the box hadn't been disturbed for several hundred years. I couldn't remember where I was but I felt the sword at my side. I jumped from the box with the sheathed sword in one hand, my sword hand gripping the hilt. I was prepared to draw, to lop off heads, but everyone in the room bent the knee and bowed heads. Evidently there had been rumors of a famous knight traveling to the area: they thought I was he, and brought me to a local leader."

"The language wasn't something I was able to understand, but ultimately I deciphered that they had brought me to some Gaulish king, the greatest warrior of his day, for the purpose of joining his army. The king's name was Charles, Charles the Hammer, they call him in history classes today, and this man needed exceptional swords. I learned horsemanship under

Charles, and also acquired a fine broadsword to replace the blade I had slept with. But the blade wasn't enough for me, so I traveled north again."

"I heard Ragnar Lodbrok was building an Army, so I went to him. Just as Charles had been, Ragnar was happy to have an exceptional sword. Although Ragnar was assassinated shortly after I met him, I traveled with his sons to England, and enjoyed many great battles there."

"The broad sword I had acquired was a fine blade, and it kept me happy for a time, although I found it somewhat clumsy in spite of my strength. I had taken to contemplating my box opening experience, and considered the shock of the opening. Perhaps I can make some kind of device to open a box after a hundred or two hundred years, I thought. So I traveled south, to a place called St Albans Monastery, where people were paying attention to this thing called time."

"Ultimately, however, I grew tired of this new challenge, and I found another basement sanctuary. St

Paul's Cathedral, they called it. I prepared a crypt, a box and a strong lock on the door. Then I went to sleep."

"When was that?" Vanessa asked.

"I guess you would call it 860 or 875 AD."

"So you were only able to tolerate several hundred years before another sleeping?"

Sessai held his chin. "Sometimes life is like… what is it the old Americans call it?.. a broken record? And this St Paul's Cathedral, the crypt there seemed quite secure. I might have slept five hundred years there if it weren't for a fire."

"A fire?" Vanessa asked, remembering Warsaw.

"Yes, I broke out of my box and out of that secure crypt in 1087 AD because St Paul's burned down. I spent the next several hundred years with the monks of St Albans studying clocks, and there made the timed lock that I used with your father's box near Poltava."

"One thousand AD. Twelve hundred AD. You didn't meet my father until almost seventeen hundred AD."

"You are a good student, Vanessa," Sessai replied. "I became bored with clocks and locks after several hundred years, and decided to begin my search again for the perfect blade. I took a chest with some armor, my broadsword and the new clock/lock, and found the silk road. It wasn't too hard to hire on as a guard with some merchants, so soon I was learning about silk."

"Of course, the Mongol merchants were quite sensitive about the details of the silk, and I wasn't so much interested in them. When I heard a rumor, that the best swords in the world were made in a place you today call Japan, across the sea, I found a boat and went there. I found a crypt in Okazaki castle, set my lock for a hundred years, and had another sleeping."

"Thanks to my clock/lock and a better understanding of the local language, when I awoke, I passed as a wandering samurai and took the name I still use today."

"Which is?" Vanessa asked. "Taigen Sessai," he replied.

"Enough history," Stefan almost shouted. "We have work to do," he said with a smile and glance at his daughter.

##

She watched them land from a vantage point at the pilot's lounge, one at a time. Amazed that this was actually happening. A squadron of A-10's from America. Just for her and her pilots. A miracle, to be sure. She wondered how much the aircraft performance would match the simulators. Wondered what kind of condition these aircraft would be in.

Aircraft after aircraft landed. Her ground crews guided them to spots where they were safe. These armored huts wouldn't save them from a full assault, she knew, but at least they provided temporary protection from prying Russian UAV's and sporadic artillery fire, if those came.

They were here, we were risking the threat of war, because we were worried. We were worried, and the

Americans were worried too, that those UAV's just might come.

"Smith. Fancy meeting you here."

She turned to face Major Joel Stein. "Stein. Amazing the air force kept you so long," Vanessa deadpanned in reply. 6'5", jet black hair. Major's rank. Still a cocky bastard.

"How did you make rank so fast? And… A10's? That's a bit of a come down for you, isn't it? I thought you were flying F35's." Vanessa raised her eyebrows.

"Just a transport pilot. In truth, I'm responsible for the squadron of F16's in Kiev. Six month tour. The C-130 to take my crew back to Kiev arrives in an hour. Want to see the Warthogs?"

"Sure," she answered. And off they walked.

##

How is it most of the world has forgotten that Belorussia is still Communist? Much like the hermit kingdom in Korea, a secretive state with a cult of personality around its leader. Olya met several of his family. The one boy anyone might accurately call crown prince of the nation, took an interest in her.

Taking an interest has a unique meaning with a crown prince. In all human societies, a crown prince has what he wants. Olya's ability to flirt, control, invite, then find him another interest, might have been risky. Of course, she was well coached. In one year, she met Sergey Kuzovlev, commander of the 58th Guards Army and understanding its reinforcement of Ukraine rebels with a rocket launcher. They also talked about existing troop presence in Belorussia.

Olya met Sergey Sevryukov, commander of the 49th Guards Army (former commanders Surgey Kuralenko and Viktor Astapov).

She had even more time with Yevgeny Nikiforov, commander Russian 20th Guards Army, and his infantry division commander. A female political officer never left his side. Cleo studied Olya. She studied them all, never missing a detail.

Lunch for Stefan, Sessai and Olya in Minsk. "This has been fun," said Olya.

"But very dangerous," said Stefan.

"You have done enough," added Sessai.

"I'm fine," said Olya.

Sessai smiled. "You have done so exceptionally well. We think it's time for you to get your life back."

"You've been accepted to Virginia Tech in the Fall. If you choose, you can connect with us from time to time. We'd also like to introduce you to Vanessa."

Olya wondered if she should confess. Ultimately, she thought it a good idea. "She and I have met."

Sessai and Stefan exchanged glances. "When?"

"A few years ago. I went to Baltimore to meet her."

It hadn't come up. "How did it go?"

"Fine," answered Olya.

"Well, we think you should see her again, then. Consider it part of your out briefing. Best if you don't talk about the Belorussian phase of your life with anyone, other than the three of us."

##

"Understand you two have met," said Sessai as he walked into Stefan's apartment. Behind Sessai was Vanessa's twin. Vanessa smiled. "Hi Olya. What have you told him?"

"Only that I'm fortunate you didn't report me." Her expression was sober. Sessai and Stefan exchanged glances. "Yes, you might have been staffing a small Ukraine chocolate shop for the rest of your sweet life."

"Instead I've been helping you keep Belorussia on your side."

"Let's not exaggerate your role too much."

Olya shrugged. "I'm not over emphasizing what I've done. A few polite dates with the crown prince (she winked at Vanessa), but mostly just maintaining the good will you and Stefan built with that vodka. In any event, I believe Russian troops and tanks in Belorussia will be mired in traffic or stuck behind locked gates if attacks come from elsewhere."

"That is as much as we can ask," whispered Stefan.

##

"I am a professional. Your rationale is none of my business." Her contact changed the subject, with small talk. Putin's solid standing. Communism continuing in Belorussia. A new government, the Orange Revolution, in Ukraine.

Litvinienko, the squeaky wheel in London.

"You are asking me to get some low-level bureaucrat?" asked Cleo. "It should make you angry, that that guy would lie so badly about our great motherland."

Cleo pondered her reply. "In any event, you aren't paying me enough. I understand he isn't as dangerous a target, but I'm no pauper. I don't work for these rates."

He shrugged in reply. "This is what we need."

"I want the primary political officer job with the 20th Guards."

His eyebrows went up. "Very unusual request."

"I am ready for something a bit more stable," Cleo said.

"Let me see what I can do. Probably the best we will get you is in the 3rd MRD."

"I will take the job if you offer me that."

##

They hired Cleo as a waitress at the restaurant where Litvinienko ate. On three separate occasions, she laced his food. Eventually Litvinienko died, although it wasn't a pleasant death. Or a quick one.

Nor was it quiet, from a political perspective. Everyone accused the Russian regime.

No one accused Cleo. She left for Russia, where they issued her a uniform and introduced her to a humble office near the rest of the staff of the 3rd Motorized Rifle Division, 20th Tank Guards Army.

##

Next came Cleo's training. There were meetings. The importance of the political officer's job. Briefings about Khrushchev work as a military political officer during the birth of the Soviet Union. His work as a military political officer during the Great Patriotic War. Of course, Khrushchev's strength, standing up to the great devil in the West.

"Efficiency and diligence," training underscored. Keeping a tight eye on command and staff. For years, alcohol had been a problem. Tracking substance abuse within the command had grown in importance after the Soviet Union was replaced with a Confederation of Independent States. Although assessing loyalty to Russia was important, determining whether leadership were good communists was not part of the mission, any longer.

##

At a restaurant near the airport in Minsk, Stefan, Olya and Sessai enjoyed another meal. "Show her the drawing," interjected Stefan.

"What are the odds?" asked Sessai.

"This is an international manhunt. I'm frankly surprised you haven't shown it to her before now."

"She has done enough, and done it brilliantly. Cleo would have only been a distraction."

"Cleo?" asked Olya.

Sessai showed her a crime scene pencil drawing based on a two-hundred-year-old set of recollections from the two vampires in the room.

"Of course. This is the political officer of the 3rd MRD. Is that a test?"

"What?" Neither Sessai nor Stefan would have guessed that Cleo would have found a home within the Russian ground forces. They wondered how long she had been there, each simultaneously, but not breathing a word of that question to Olya.

"How do you know? Are you sure?"

"I told you I met the leadership of the 20th Guards Army. Pretty sure I mentioned the 3rd MRD. The political officer is a flunky, an annoying hindrance, not really a contributor to tactics or strategy, although certainly someone linked into the goings of unit, and ties to political leadership in Moscow."

"Do we really think this is a good drawing?" asked Sessai. "I think it's pretty good." Said Stefan.

"Okay Olya. You leave tonight."

Not before the party at the Overtime, thought Olya.

The Overtime Nightclub was a massive structure in the center of Minsk. Olya arrived late, but never had to wait to get in, thanks to connections to the ruling family. They weren't with her this night, but other friends were there. She danced with girlfriends, a few boys and men that fancied something more from her, momentary or maybe longer lasting.

Flashing lights, loud music. Lady Gaga, Justin Bieber, Katie Perry. Who was it? She just remembered the smiling faces, adoring the music, dancing so single mindedly, then there was that kiss.

Oh yes, that kiss. Exploring hands.

She tried to leave. He followed her. She wanted him to. There was more kissing.

Then she slipped into the woman's room. Quickly escaped to a cab outside.

Went home to sleep. Packed her bag. Caught her plane.

She didn't flirt with the pilot.

She read a book. The Book of Joy. Dalai Lama and Desmond Tutu. She read a magazine. A newspaper.

There was a layover in Frankfurt. More reading, no flirting. Lots of reading, a movie, some sleeping.

She stepped off the airplane at Dulles International Airport in Virginia. No Mom and Dad. No Tom. No airline pilot. But in the Fall, there would be Virginia Tech, and with it, a long, happy life staring at her. "That's my story, and I'm sticking to it," thought Olya.

##

The young guard who stopped her most mornings stopped her again that morning. Cleo had uncharacteristically skipped the t-shirt under her uniform. Of course, the young man saw her cleavage. She told him her address and asked if he knew where the address was. She handed him a scrap of paper, with her address scrawled on it.

"When do you get off?" she asked.

"1830, ma'am," said the young man. "You better arrive at my place no later than 1930. Is that clear?" she asked him. "Yes Ma'am," he answered, blushing.

She was waiting in a lace robe when he arrived. "So sweet," she said, kissing him passionately, ignoring his exploring hands.

Cleo pursed her lips, ending the kiss, and gazed into the boy's crazed eyes. She smiled and bit into his neck.

##

The boy brought ten of his friends the next week. They sat in the living room, with completely the wrong impression regarding what would happen when they went into the room to visit her. Each had detailed instructions when they left her presence, walking straight to the front door and departing to fulfill those orders. Detailed instructions and open cuts on the neck.

Three months later, Cleo had vampies throughout the 3rd MRD. She kept the boy as her lover. Isis was right about that.

##

"You wanted to see me, sir," Cleo stated, walking into the offices of the commander, third Motorized Rifle Division. He was a man on the rise, but he had heard rumors.

"They say you have been a bit active in my ranks," he asked her. She is attractive, he thought. Hmm.

"Active, sir?" Cleo asked. She was certain her meetings caught his attention, but all her vampies were sworn to secrecy.

"What are you doing with those boys, Pol?"

"Just doing my job, sir." She answered.

None of them would talk about what happened. He suspected it was something sexual. Wouldn't be the first time. Yet finances for all of them seemed fine. Whatever was happening, they weren't paying for it. "And what is your job? Perhaps we can review." he asked her.

"Insuring loyalty and efficiency, sir."

"Tell me how you do that." Her commander ordered.

"Surely you would be surprised if your commander requested details of your methods."

"Perhaps, once I have established his confidence, such a request would surprise me. But you and I are only recently acquainted, and, if I understand correctly, this tactical assignment is a new experience for you."

"Have you received problematic reports, sir?" she asked her boss.

He took a breath and studied her demeanor. Impeccable uniform. Nothing untoward, only his suspicions. "Do I have an evil mind?" wondered the commander. "No." He answered. "See that I don't."

"You won't sir." She paused. "Will that be all, sir?"

"That will be all."

"Thank you," responded Cleo. She stood, saluted, and went back to the meeting schedule she had planned.

##

General Redgrave arrived with her team.… There were many details to arrange. Specifications to confirm with factories in Karkhiv. Inventories to produce, for testing here, and perhaps shipment to the United States later. There were also railheads to coordinate, for a brigade that would be stationed in Karkhiv and a Regiment that would be stationed around Zhytomyr.

##

Vanessa's phone rang. She picked up to a voice she hadn't heard in some time. "Ma'am, it's so great to hear from you!" Vanessa told her old boss.

Redgrave told her about the plant upgrades in Kharkiv, and the timeline for parts inventories. She mentioned the US funding that had been required, and the prestigious banks that were involved. Then she said, "There is someone here who wants to talk with you."

A man's voice came on the phone. "Vanessa," the man said, "unsure if you will remember me, but we were classmates at Leonard Wood. Hank Reardon."

She thought for a moment, and inhaled. "Tall, kind of wiry. Sandy hair?"

"That's right. Good memory. Listen, I hoped we might do dinner tonight."

She shook her head. "Umm. You are in Kiev. I am in Zhytomir. That's a problem. I have access to jet aircraft," she said, laughing quietly, "but I can't exactly pop into your neighborhood."

"Well," he answered. "I also have access to a jet, and," he added, glancing at General Redgrave, "I can come to you. Meet me on the Zhytomir tarmac at 5pm? Can you pick a restaurant?"

"Sure. See you there." The line went dead. Vanessa remembered Hank. Scrawny guy. Barely passed his PT test. "This is going to be interesting," she thought to herself.

She was leaning against her ZAZ when his plane touched down. Lear… smooth lines. Nicer than anything the Army had in inventory. When the stairs hit ground and the door opened, a wiry man in a suit and overcoat stepped out, glanced around, then walked purposely down the stairs and toward her.

Vanessa walked around the passenger side and opened the door. "You look better in a suit than you did in a uniform," she smiled wryly. "Thanks," he said, smiling in return. He knew it to be true. He climbed in the car and she shut the door.

After dinner she was approaching his hotel, when he asked if she would come up. "I have something to show you," he had said. "Here we go," Vanessa thought. But she agreed.

Inside his room, he had stepped into the bathroom and she walked to the small table near the TV. On it, was a scrap book, opened to an article about her bronze star. The smiling picture. She started to read when he stepped up behind her. She turned and he handed her a rose. He had removed the suit jacket and tie, rolled up his sleeves. Wiry, chopped hair, sparkling eyes.

"Kind of creepy," she said, motioning to the scrap book. He laughed. "Yes, I have been stalking you since OBC." She smelled the rose.

"You made a good impression. I usually didn't date people who could beat me up, but…" he touched her cheek, "so beautiful. And," he added, motioning to the scrap book, "so impressive."

He kissed her. She let him.

##

The ACR logistics officer had loaded the M1's from dry storage with elements from each of the squadrons. The team had received detailed instructions from Gen Redgrave's staff regarding upgrades, especially the UAV guns, and had already been coordinating for installation not far from the airport.

When the Regimental Commander arrived, the full command and staff were on hand to troop level. It had been many years since the Second Armored Cavalry Regiment had deployed as a true ACR, and to have the veteran of Little Easting in charge of the Regiment added electricity to the moment. No one but the commander had served with the ACR in those days, but everyone had been to the museum.

"Take your seats," said Col McMaster, after he walked to the head of the room.

##

Like stars in a galaxy, the battalions of the 26th were assigned to Zolochiv, Staryi Saltiv, Chuhuiv and Lisne. But the leadership of the 26th Infantry Brigade met with General Redgrave and her team near the railhead in Kharkiv. The Commander and his Command Sergeant Major, along with all his staff. The Commanders of 1/31, 1/81 and 1/104. Each battalion had command sergeant major and full complement of staff, except the 1/81, who were missing the command sergeant major and Battalion S2.

1/81 S2 and sergeant major were moving from site to site, pouring concrete onto steel lattice, and digging holes that might accommodate Bradleys and Abrams for the companies of the battalion. When each of the companies arrived, First Sergeants were there to direct traffic. All vehicles were secure from threat of that first Russian volley, the S2 had endeared himself to his troop commanders and the battalion commander had secured his "one block" under Mullaly. Although a Soldier is never ready, 1/81 was ready.

Shortly thereafter, the other battalions of the 26th had overhead cover also. The brigade truck company began making parts deliveries to the F-16 squadron in Kiev, the 2d ACR at Zaporizhia and the A10 squadron at Kryvyi Rih.

##

Vanessa arrived at Rucker mid-afternoon on a Sunday. She went immediately from the airport to her storage unit and broke into her uniforms. "Thank you for small miracles," she said to herself as she loaded her items into the rental car and drove onto the base to report to the aviation school.

Her phone began to buzz. "Hi Hank. Thanks for calling." He was calling to coordinate his trip for the following weekend. Wondering if he should get a hotel or stay with her.

"I will still be in a hotel, but will plan to get a larger room for next weekend. Perhaps you can help me move into my new place next Sunday."

"Perhaps," he said, smiling. Perhaps.

##

The Armored Cavalry Regiment was deployed like a mantis, Squadron headquarters claws near Balaklya and Lozova, mirrored at Pokrovske and Tokmak. The aviation squadron, mouth of the beast, collocated with Regimental Headquarters at Zaporizya(or was it with the A10's at Krivyi Rih?).

Maneuver in Ukraine

Life really isn't about merit. Doesn't matter what you know, or what skills you have. Doesn't even matter who you know. What matters is what you can apply. What you can apply, where people want (or can be forced) to credit you with your work.

Vanessa Smith was watching the waves off the Outer Banks, North Carolina, United States of America, pondering the questions that a surfer faces. Which wave shall I ride? How shall I catch it? Do I have the skills to ride it where it will go, and if not, can I do anything about that now?

She was standing on the sun-bleached porch of a little beach chalet, sipping a cappuccino made by one of those new-fangled coffee machines that let you choose whatever you want to drink. Your own little barista, plugged into the power in your kitchen, connected to your home network or mobile phone, so you can even instruct the thing to prepare you something when you aren't around to push the buttons yourself.

Hank stepped up behind her, wrapped his arms around her waist and kissed her neck. "Much nicer to have a warm, willing to please, barista in residence." She turned to him and kissed him back. Together they watched an osprey, hovering above the water, hunting for fish. It dove, but emerged without quarry.

"Time flies," he said. She nodded, a bit sad. A short break from the Army. Yes, she won her wings, and orders for the Second Armored Cavalry Regiment in Ukraine. But would she be stuck in an S3 air role at Regimental Headquarters, or even worse, sent to some Ukraine maneuver or government headquarters where her Russian might help McMaster more than her budding tactical and piloting skills might, at the moment?

She turned to Hank, wondering if she would see him again. So many options for him in New York City. She felt something pushing against her, and let her hand move to explore his pajamas. "You fly," she said, smiling mischievously.

The osprey dove again, this time emerging from the water with a fish in its claws. "That bird isn't going to let go," thought Vanessa. Her fingers found the back of Hank's fuzzy hair and she kissed him again, more passionately this time.

##

He stood watching her check her bags. Two big green duffle bags and a wider canvas tote. She clutched the camouflage purse he had purchased from that custom shop for her… perhaps a bit more feminine than standard Army or surplus store options, but still camouflage. She loved it, laughing and kissing, when he gave it to her. He wondered whether he would see her again as she waved, then she turned and walked to the gate. Perhaps he should have bought her that diamond ring…

Vanessa handed her ticket to the United employee at the gate. No time to spare. "Oh, you have been upgraded to first class," said the pretty brunette. "Well… thank you." Vanessa wondered whether that was Hank, the airline, or some other kind passenger.

She walked down the tunnel to the aircraft, then found her seat at the window. She could see Hank waving at the window. She waved back, unsure he would be able to see her. It all seemed like such a miracle.

##

Colonel McMaster was surprised. "Captain Smith reporting for duty, sir."

"Your reputation precedes you," he had said. "So does yours, sir," she replied.

"Your squadron commander is Tom Bryant. One of the best warfighters in the Regiment and, they tell me, a damn fine pilot. Also, you won't get any special treatment."

"I don't expect any, sir."

"Fighting has been stiff. We didn't know what to expect in the first wave. Turns out, they had plenty of UAV's to replace the ones we shot down. Concentration of our counter UAV birds has been in the Northeast, since my M1's are also anti-UAV equipped. We are minimizing travel in thin skinned vehicles, but frankly even armor is vulnerable. Be careful."

Vanessa saluted, turned and exited his office, heading for the aviation squadron. She was looking forward to meeting Colonel Bryant, her company and her new Apache.

##

Captain Smith thought that the assumption of command in Ukraine went smoothly. The battalion property book officer understood the equipment in her troop thoroughly and prepared useful piles of paper to support the process. Troop command. Amazing. Deux ex machina?

Her platoon leaders were outstanding (fabulous US Army word) officers without exception, intrigued to follow an A-10 driver with an Iraq Bronze Star for valor on her chest. True, she was young for a troop commander, and relatively new in a helicopter. But Captain Smith's thoughts about air ambushes and the aeronautics degree from Hopkins affirmed the Army's decision to put her in that job.

McMaster liked to lead from the front. It was an old habit, and "HR" thought it kept him sharp. Many cav commanders commandeered a helicopter and called instructions from there. McMaster would ride in the 2d Squadron formation, with his tank crew modified somewhat so his tank was responsive to the lead troop commander's coordination, while McMaster himself listened to the regimental command and intelligence nets, watching the evolution of Common Operating Picture on his Google glasses from his perch in the TC's chair.

The regimental headquarters were located in Dnipropetrovsk, prepared to displace to Kremenchuck.

McMaster gave Lieutenant Colonel Artie Wyman the mission to screen between Slovyask and Svatove with 1st Squadron, including an active defense along E40 highway. Wyman was preparing to displace through Kremenchuch to Kirovohrad in a wide sweeping motion.

Lieutenant Colonel Crabchuk was screening along E40 and E50 between Slovyansk and Krasnarmisk, with 2d Squadron's center of mass at Luzova. Active defense along E50 would be supplanted with a displacement to Uman, crossing bridges at Dnipropetrovsk.

Third Squadron had the bulk of the Regimental air defense assets, where Lieutenant Colonel Tommy Isaacs was responsible for screening south of E50 and North of Polohy, defending bridges (and 2d Squadron' crossing) at Dnipropetrovsk. The squadron would be prepared to counterattack toward Kharkiv.

Lieutenant Colonel Tip Carney would repel any amphibious attacks thru Mariupol and Melitopol, screening between Zaporezhya and Nova Kakovka with 4th Squadron, east of Tokmak, North to Poloky and south to E58. The squadron would consolidate west of Zaporizhya, prepared to counterattack toward Kharkiv behind Third Squadron if that were necessary. Initial efforts for a combined arms ambush at Melitopol would complement screening efforts.

Tom Bryant's Aviation Squadron ran simulated ambush patrols from its base in Krevhi Rih to Rodisne, Vosnesensk, Vozryatski and Bashtanka, with orders to displace to Cherkavsky.

Can a part time warrior really lead a brigade in combat? Happened all the time in the US Civil War. But modern mobilizations typically give National Guard brigades less critical tasks (supplying sheets and pillows for barracks in combat zone). A National Guard armored brigade that received a combat mission for its Iraq deployment this decade had a substantial number of casualties.

In any event, the 26th Infantry brigade commander wasn't suffering from any inferiority complexes. A twenty-nine year veteran who began his career with an active duty tour with the Rangers, Mullaly had received an MBA from Boston University with his enlistment education benefit, while attending the Massachusetts National Guard OCS and BOLC. He worked as a CPA for a "big six" (big four? Big three? Big two?) accounting firm, working his way through company and battalion command.

He had moved to Virginia to serve in the Pentagon until selected for brigade command, returning for assumption of command ceremonies and paperwork three months before the deployment announcement. His unit strength was "plussed up" from National Guard units across the country, although he tended to keep his own Guard leadership in command roles up and down the chain of command.

He and his brigade flew into Ukraine for a NATO Sorotan exercise, some arriving in Kiev on commercial aircraft, others flying direct to Kharkiv on C-130 or C-123 aircraft. US equipment arrived at railheads near Kharkiv, with trucks focusing on movement of 1-81 and 1-104 "light infantry" battalions, and members of 1-72 Tank and 1-31 Infantry joining M1 and M2 tank and armored personnel equipment at railheads for movement to staging areas.

Press coverage and Russian response were ferocious. Fortunately, his soldiers weren't able to read the local Russian language news media. Mullaly selected a five-story building in the northeast quadrant of Kharkiv (Kyivsky district) for his brigade headquarters and proceeded to build his multi-media tactical operations center on the fifth floor. UAV feeds, radios, sand tables and a large auditorium for brigade ops meetings were perfect.

Lieutenant Colonel Lowjack wasn't happy to leave his manufacturing business for a NATO exercise, but he knew they wouldn't select him for brigade command if he missed this mob. He was delighted with the initiative of his command sergeant major and intel officer, who had prepared concrete bunkers for the anti-tank missile vehicles.

Defending in depth at Stary Saltiv would not be an easy mission if the Russians ever came across. Of course, the Donets river was a fantastic obstacle, which he would easily defend once any attacking forces made it through the web of A company strong points and battalion antitank missiles pointed down the avenues of approach enroute to that beautiful bridge his infantry would preserve if possible.

With the other three companies of the 1-81 infantry battalion on the western side of Donets, Lojack was sure he would offer disaster to any air assault or air mobile operation between Stary Saltiv and Kharkiv.

Lieutenant Colonel Moredone was responsible for coordinating with the Ukrainian mechanized infantry division located southeast of Kharkiv and preventing penetration of threat forces northwest of the intersection at Chuhuiv. Defending in depth as his plan, which was integrated in a thorough defense of the airfield west of Chuhuiv, enabling secure refuel/rearm of US air force aircraft (mostly A10's but perhaps an occasional F15 and/or F16) there.

The 1-31 Mechanized Infantry battalion was responsible for coordinating with the Ukrainian tank division headquartered at Cheringov, and configured with two companies forward (one just south of Berezivka, the other just north of Zolochiv, on the other side of the westward bend in the road there) and two companies in reserve (one just southeast of Zolochiv while the other company were prepared to defend or reposition on the edge of the woods there).

Lieutenant Colonel Tielilly configured the 1-72 Tank Battalion with two companies forward (one north of Lisne, the other southeast of Cherkaska Lozova) and two companies in reserve (slightly northwest of Turkuny, in the tree line, and one south of the E105/E40, vicinity the bend in E105). He was prepared to dispatch a company sized tank force to reinforce the 1-104 should an attack from Belorus not materialize.

##

Rodisne, Vosnesensk, Vozryatski and Bashtanka. Alpha troop, Bravo troop, Charlie and Delta. Vanessa glanced at her ops lieutenant and First Sergeant. The lieutenant smiled at her… he had predicted that objective and had already begun coordination for the air corridors to get them there. First Sergeant Dominion only frowned.

Colonel Bryant was predicting where the Russian main effort might come, options for refueling and rearming in event of outbreak, and how the simulation would work these next few days. "Any questions?" he asked. Bravo troop commander asked something mildly pertinent to prove he was listening. After saluting, Captain Smith turned and left the office with her troop leadership.

Bryant turned to his Sergeant Major after they all left for planning activities. "Any issues?" His advisor shook his head. "No sir."

The Colonel smiled. "Then let's get to work planning our support for Fourth Squadron's Melitopol ambush."

##

"What is your estimate, two?" Colonel Mullaly was studying large maps including Belorussia, Russia and Ukraine. His Operations Officer, Lieutenant Colonel Fitzgo, had just been outlining company positions for each of the battalions of the brigade. His Intelligence Officer, Major Whysmartie, suggested, "If we see anyone, I believe it will be elements of the 20th Guards, probably the 3rd Rifle Division."

Mullaly glanced at his "three," the Ops officer, then told Whysmartie, "you need to be more certain than that."

Major Whysmartie smiled. "We can expect three infantry brigades and a separate tank brigade from the 3rd MRD, supported by an artillery brigade, two rocket brigades and two anti-aircraft rocket brigades. We think the 58th Guards will snatch Kiev, leaving Karkhiv to the 20th and its 3rd MRD. The 49th Army is oriented south of us.

"Pretty overwhelming," responded Mullaly. Fitzgo chimed in, "We will have dedicated support from the F-16's based in Kharkiv."

"What about A-10's?" Mullaly wondered.

"Those will probably be oriented in the Donbass and supporting the 2d ACR against the 49th."

"There is a chance the 20th will bypass us completely and support the 58th grab of Kiev." Wouldn't that be nice, thought Whysmartie.

"What do you think about that, three?" wondered the commander.

"I think we're going to have a fight on our hands, mostly coming from the north, not the east." Fitzgo spit in his soda can.

"I think you're right," responded Mullaly. "Adjust the plan. I want 1-31 and 1-72 to be two balanced Infantry/Armor task forces, but then I want one of TF 1-72's companies attached to 1-81's A Company commander, who I'm going to task with defending Karkhiv just within city limits." Fitzgo nodded. "Tielilly will be pissed about that," he mentioned with a smile.

Deadpan, Mullaly answered, "Needs of the Army."

##

Vanessa was flying her apache south along the Crimean Sea. Her boss, Lieutenant Colonel Bryant, was wedged in the back seat with the Regimental Intel Officer, Major McKrockcity. Colonel McMaster was sitting in the co-pilot seat. McKrockcity was talking.

"There is a chance the 20th will mass through Donbass to grab Dnipropetrovsk, but I think it's more likely they will stay in place and we will see airmobile/airborne operations to support a 58th Guards Army attack on Kiev." As they flew over Melitipol, Colonel Bryant said, "If they attempt a beach assault around here, a 4th Squadron combined arms ambush can count on Captain Vanessa's support."

"I think we need to be very prepared to place half of the Regiment south of Kiev to counter-attack on a successful 58th Army grab of Kiev, and half attacking North to retake Kharkiv from the 20th. But if the 49th Guards come at Dnipropetrovsk from Donbass and," he added, "or North across the water, we will be ready." McMaster was grim. He wasn't comfortable with the rocket arsenal and UAV fleet he knew would be directing fire on his Regiment, if the Russians decided to take back Ukraine.

"Roger, sir."

##

Rada Verkhovna. People's power.

Stefan Cossack had been intrigued with Ukraine's democracy since attending the Dnieper Cossack's Rada with Ivan Mazeppa, shortly after the unification of East and West banks. Mazeppa had waxed poetic about democracy in the Hetmanate, even if he wasn't willing to vest it with full powers.

Mazeppa had hoped to establish a broader body, such as the one existing today, to bring consensus to the Hetmanate across a number of topics. Unfortunately, resources and blood required to support the Tsar's wars had shortened patience with his own petty nobility. Then, with the time it took for Peter the Great to move a large army, time ran out for Mazeppa.

If contemplating the history of the Rada was a complicated topic, getting elected to it was something else altogether.

Stefan thought "Deputy Cossack" had a nice ring to it, and that 2016 election was a crowning accomplishment after his 1917 and 1919 efforts to reestablish democracy in Ukraine were quashed by the Russian Communists. Even waving Mazeppa's sword, Stefan's credibility was limited in those days.

Why does democracy matter, anyhow? In America, with its claim to the longest running one, critics of the new President seem to alternatively want to take the reins of government away from this crazy system or mourn that Trump will do so. Some contemplate how much more efficient the United States government would be if the separation of powers ceased to exist.

Others observe subtle (and perhaps not so subtle) favoritism advances the interests of the wealthy, some races over others, men over women, some sexual preferences over others. Equal justice under the law... is that even a goal anymore? It does seem most attempt to advocate for advantages for their own group, not equality for all.

Power corrupts. Absolute power corrupts absolutely, they say. Yet democracy in many places hasn't eliminated corruption. Korea's leader resigns due to improprieties. Some of the most vicious criticisms of modern Ukraine focus on corruption, with dramatic recent examples almost made possible through democratic elections of people with less than savory objectives.

Stefan was thankful for the financial resources Sessai brought, remembering the financial success he enjoyed before the kulaks lost everything. "They say I have a sense of entitlement," he mused.

The debate was about funding for various Ukraine units. Oligarchs paid for some, while others received pay/benefits from the state. Best case, the state of the Ukraine economy since Russia had occupied Donbass and Crimea suffered, although it might be accurate to observe we just failed to capitalize on early momentum enjoyed just after the Soviet Union dissolved.

Stefan was familiar with Russian accusations that natural gas and oil were stolen from the pipelines. "Druzhba," those pipes were called. Hmm. People were freezing...

The chairman recognized Stefan's raised hand. "Thank you for the opportunity to address my esteemed colleagues, Mr. Chairman," said Stefan. "We must establish standard pay scales for all our military, and insure they are independent bodies, such as militaries in all western democracies. We have come too far to continue to appear, or even be in fact, a collection of squabbling warlords."

"I move that we vote to absorb all the military organizations within the Ukraine Department of Defense, standardize rank, benefits and authorities, and make other activities illegal."

"Second," shouted several his colleagues. "We will need legislation to that effect," said the chairman. Indeed, thought Stefan. A worthy effort....

##

No plan survives first contact with the enemy. Just at the end of the Russian's annual Kavkaz exercises that year, Russian forces began landing on the Ukraine coast, massing in Crimea/Donbass and across the Russian border from Kiev and Kharkiv. News reports suggested water shortages in Kharkiv and Dnipropetrovsk, while the Russian press were claiming the Ukraine wasn't even able to manage its water supply, based on reports.

"What water shortages?" wondered Colonel Mullaly as he filled his glass at the sink in the fifth floor bathroom. "Tastes fine too," he mused.

But his "two" was briefing the location of subordinate units of the 3rd MRD, massing on the border. "This might not be such a good building to be in," said the "two" at the conclusion of his briefing. "There are thousands of Twitter and other social media claims about poisoned or scarce water in Kharkiv and Dnipropetrovsk," he added. "The outside world evidently thinks Ukrainians are dying of thirst."

##

Chief of the Civil Military Administration from Donbass was briefing the Rada. "If we allow the Russians to seize the rest of the country, they will shut down plants and large businesses everywhere as they have in Donbass these past years.

Stefan wasn't happy with the state of the Ukraine economy without Russian occupation, but clearly, ramifications of a broader take-over were dire indeed. "Why does Russia want more desert?" he wondered.

The next speaker talked about the Russian 44th Training Tank Regiment. The 1st Army Corps. The 2d

Army Corps. He mentioned the T90 tanks of the 136th Motorized Rifle Brigade and wondered how many units had been upgraded with these state-of-the-art tanks.

Stefan hoped the Americans were tracking these developments.

He and Sessai had been talking the other day about Cleo and the 3rd MRD. "Do you think there will be vampies?" he asked.

"I am certain of it," answered Sessai. "The question isn't 'will there be,' but 'how many will there be?'"

Stefan thought for a moment. "We need to share this with Vanessa."

He knew better than to worry about his daughter, but he was excited at the prospect of leaving parliamentary debate to return to a battlefield.

##

Radar identified the little bird for what it was: harbinger of death. The operator engaged before his report went in, but the CO wanted confirmation before he would report to higher. 2d PL/B Squadron took the radio: "Roger sir, I have seen the wreckage myself."

"You just engaged 5 minutes ago."

"Roger sir. It was definitely a Russian UAV."

##

The 26th wasn't as well equipped, although they found overhead cover under the concrete and steel shelters when barrages came in. They, meaning most everyone. 1/81 A's first sergeant was caught in the open delivering food. A Soldier from 1/31 D had been on a smoke break. Barrages aren't forgiving…

##

The two Ukrainian Divisions were put on alert, as were the A-10's and one of the F-16 Squadrons.

##

Several Russian amphibious landings came in east of Odessa -- standard amphibious craft at Khrysanivka and several freighters that were carrying troops instead of grain, that docked at Mikolaiv.

Vanessa's air cav troop was flying low, what the army calls "nap of the earth," anticipating they would ambush the lead elements of that amphibious attack when the Russian marines arrived at Petrivka. Vanessa knew she could expect reinforcements from the troop that was stationed on ambush at Revova, assuming landings weren't successful at Odessa itself. She thought Charlie troop, sent to Voznesensk, would be busy in and around that area.

Harassing fires were nipping at 4th Squadron's western flank, near Nova Kakhovka, but Melitopol was quiet.

In any event, in the skies above, pairs of F15's were streaking past. Those were the aircraft she could see. She wondered about the aircraft she wasn't able to see.

##

"Sir, there is something over the net about a 90th Guards Tank Division." McMaster jumped out of bed. "What? Where?"

"At first we thought they were trucks, massing as a ruse. Then maybe ammunition to support some of the other activity we're seeing. But these are definitely tanks… the best the Russians have."

McMaster's M1 was waiting outside. He climbed aboard.

##

Rockets were landing on the 1-81 positions east of the Donetsk. Aircraft had strafed the 1-104th in various positions, and the airfield they were defending had been bombed. But Mullaly, now riding on a Bradley infantry fighting vehicle in southwest Kharkiv, was most worried about two infantry brigades and a separate tank brigade that had attacked across the border.

Both TF 1-31 and TF-1-72 were engaged, but withdrawing in the face of a much more numerous force. At this point, they were running low on ammunition and were headed to the reconstitution point at Lyubotyn.

##

Sessai and Stefan were watching headquarters vehicles from the 3rd MRD from a UAV feed. Three men and a woman— a brunette —exited the vehicles and entered the building that had been the 26th Infantry Brigade's headquarters. They zoomed the feed to the woman.

"Cleo," they muttered simultaneously, watching infantry take cover outside and in various buildings in the perimeter around the headquarters. "With her retinue of vampies," added Sessai.

##

"Toward E40, sir?" asked the driver.

"No. We need to get across the Dnipr. Head for Okeksandrivka." Answered McMaster. As they cleared the bridge over the Sarara, radar detected a UAV overhead. Electronics confirmed Russian. The tank made a "brrrp," sound, answered by a pop and a flash in the sky.

"Lobster six, this is Dragon six. Headed your way. Trust you are watching massing of the 90th, over." Lobster calmly replied, "Roger Dragon. Confirming massing and sporadic UAV overflights."

"Take all confirmed Russian UAV's. They are in our space, over." Lobster responded, "Roger, over."

"Dragon out."

McMaster glanced at his loader and switched nets to the country logistics net. "Mantis 4 this is Dragon six, over."

"Roger, Dragon. Go ahead." She answered.

"We're going to need that refuel, resupply at Yuevileine. Trust you are tracking the 90th Tank division, over."

"Roger, Dragon."

"We will send any surviving elements of 1st and 2d Squadrons to join the Air Cav Squadron resisting amphibious and any air mobile/assault operations in Western Ukraine. These elements will be under the Air Cav squadron, Wasp six."

"Roger, Dragon. Good copy. If necessary they need to support re-taking Kiev. If Mullaly is still alive, he will command US forces in that operation. Otherwise, Wasp six will command and coordinate, over."

"Roger, Mantis. I will stay with 3rd and 4th squadrons with an air cav troop, and retake Kharkiv, if necessary, over."

"Roger Dragon. Link up with elements of 1-81 and 1-104 vicinity east of and defending Kharkiv. I have the green tab in country, confirmed with Real Estate six, over."

"Roger, Mantis. Confirm you have the con."

"Roger, out."

##

"We had nothing to do with removing your troop from the rest of the Combat Aviation Squadron," Stefan was saying.

"What sort of pull do you imagine we have?" added Sessai.

Vanessa frowned. She had been cut away from the rest of her squadron to support an attack on Kharkiv, and now these two men were telling her they hoped she would allow her second in command to manage things for a few days. "We believe you can manage Cleo, where we probably cannot."

She listened to stories about Cleo's super-human strength… even beyond Vanessa's. Cleo, Cleo, Cleo, they kept telling her about Cleo. The thousand-year sleeping, which at this point was ended hundreds of years ago. They suggested Vanessa duel Cleo with two blades, while Sessai and Stefan come from either side, to her rear.

There was a back pack of super-strong chains, in the event Vanessa's swordsmanship was adequate to disarm her opponent, and the three of them were able to hold her down.

##

"Copper 6, this is Dragon 6. FRAGO, over." McMaster had jumped onto First Squadron's command net.

"Roger, Dragon 6. Prepared to copy."

"Attach fifty percent of your surviving force to Lobster 6, with travel commencing ASAP. Anticipated refuel re-supply for them at Yuevileine. I will replenish your remaining force forward, over.

"Roger Dragon 6. Will coordinate passage of lines and linkup points for detached force with Lobster 6, over."

"Roger. Screen north to eliminate T-90's in sector and support 1-104 defenses. Comms channels are available via Dragon 8.

"WILCO, Dragon."

"Dragon out."

##

"Lobster 6, this is Dragon 6. FRAGO, over."

"Roger Dragon 6. Prepared to copy."

"Accept attachment forces from Copper 6 and proceed to Yuevileine for rearm/refuel. Coordinate passage of lines with Sunglasses 6. Upon completion of rearm/refuel, proceed across the Dnipr at Dnipropetrovsk, reporting to Wasp 6 to support his combined arms ambushes in the western corridor NLT noon tomorrow. How copy, over."

"Copy rearm/refuel today with elements of Copper 6, coordinating passage with Sunglasses 6, today. Confirm orders to support Wasp 6 combat operations after crossing at Dnipropetrovsk, November Lima Tango noon tomorrow. Always ready sir."

"Toujours Pret. Dragon out."

##

"Sunglasses 6, this is Dragon 6. FRAGO, over."

"Roger, Dragon."

"Defend north and east of Yuevileine. Lobster elements will pass through your lines later today. Effective passage of lines, I will join your formation, over."

"Roger, Dragon. We will serve an anvil to any force that believes they have us in a route, over."

"Upon passage of lines, we will support Copper and Blue-Grey elements to develop the battlefield north to Kharkiv. Airborne 6 will be regimental reserve.

"Roger, Dragon."

"Dragon 6 out."

##

"Wasp 6, Dragon 6. FRAGO, over."

"Roger, Dragon. Go ahead, over."

"Lobster 6 will cross into your sector no later than tomorrow, to support your combined arms ambushes of the 61st Marine and 200th Motorized. Screen for Spetsnaz landings throughout your sector north to Kiev. Be prepared to support a counter-attack on Kiev in two days."

"Good copy Dragon. Over."

"Dragon 6 out."

##

General Redgrave met Col Mullaly at Lyubotyn. They walked to an office while he briefed her on the attack of the 3rd MRD and 136th Motorized Rifle Brigade. "We lost a lot of men," Mullaly added. "Any issues with cutting the 1-81 and 1-104 to the 2d Cav?" Redgrave wondered.

"No ma'am."

"We need you to help secure Borispol outside Kiev. NATO forces are arriving there at the end of the week."

"That's quite a drive."

"Ukrainian forces are awaiting your passage of lines."

"Okay."

She looked at the man. Clearly, he was tired. Sad, many men and women were lost. Perhaps also disappointed in losing his old battalion, indeed half of his brigade, either to the Russians or, with less bloodshed, to the 2d CAV.

"Kiev is the heart of this country. With NATO involvement, the world is with us."

"Yes, ma'am."

"What you don't know is that more than half of the ACR is west of the Dnipr, blocking 61st Marine and 200th Motorized Rifle attacks north. They are also finding Spetznaz landing points and eliminating any 'behind-the-lines' activity."

"We hope," said Mullaly.

She ignored his pessimism. "Your defense of Borispol has become the most important effort in this fight, until the arrival of NATO's Rapid Reaction Force. Do you understand?"

"It's a long drive, Ma'am."

She ignored that too. "The elements of the 2d Cav west of the Dnipr will support your retaking and defense of Borispol. Tom Bryant, the Air Cav Squadron commander, is responsible for all of them. Here is his command net. He knows he works for you." Redgrave handed Col Mullaly a scrap of paper with a radio frequency scrawled on it.

Mullaly was speechless. "That will be all," she said.

Mullaly mumbled "Yes Ma'am," in shock, saluted and left to plan the move, attack and defense of Borispol.

##

Rehearsals, rehearsals, rehearsals. Vanessa committed the details to memory: the timing of her helicopter support, the location to land, and the route to the building.

Weapons to use with the humans and vampies. The Ukraine team that would blow doors and clear the stairs. Reviewing with Stefan and Sessai how they expected a sword duel would progress. If Vanessa were able to disarm the monster, they would chain her. If not, Sessai and Stefan would approach her from the rear, opposite sides. The goal, of course, was decapitation.

##

There were two pockets, one for each sword. She recognized the blades as products of the best Japanese workmanship, long extinct. Glancing at Sessai, who would never before part with these, she put the map with graphics in her pocket and gathered the felt wrapped blades in her arms. After a glance at her father and Sessai, Vanessa turned for the door.

##

Her apache waited for her on the tarmac like a wasp with wet wings. Vanessa buckled the seatbelts around them lifted her helmet and pulled it open to slide her hair and head inside. She slid into the seat, fastened her seatbelts also, then began the start-up sequence.

##

The memory was a blur. Arriving near that building in Kharkiv and engaging vampies with her Gatling gun. Landing, more or less where they agreed. After all the dust, the vampires, the individual mortals, equipment heavy and light, she broke into the building and ran up the stairs. The door charge blew everything off, and she stepped into the dust with two swords drawn.

Sitting in the center of the room, with her sword on the ground two feet to her front, was a thin, beautiful brunette. She couldn't have been more than thirty years old… or so it appeared.

"I have waited so long to meet you," said Cleo softly.

##

Swords or Weddings

"You aren't going to believe this, Papa," Vanessa said, deadpan. Her father looked into her eyes, then beyond her to the brunette in chains. "Hello Stefan," said Cleo. The mix of emotion was overwhelming: Stefan wasn't sure whether his daughter was going to survive the encounter at all, much less intact. "How?" he wondered, glancing at Vanessa.

"I think you'll have to hear it from her." Sessai walked in the room. His rage with the chained brunette was evident. "Don't run her through with your silver until you've heard her story and we can all talk. These chains will certainly hold her until then. I've got to get back to my company."

With that, Vanessa left the room to the two old comrades and the woman they had been pursuing, who had been pursuing them, for 300 years. Cleo's eyes were wet. "I love you," she said quietly, holding Stefan's glare.

Sessai and Stefan traded glances. Sessai fingered his silver, and contemplated his promise to Vanessa.

"You are responsible for thousands of lost lives in ancient Rome. The fatalities were fewer before the Great Patriotic War, but your assistance to Hitler can also never be forgiven. Even if you were capable of tender emotions for this worthy Cossack, you certainly showed none when you met him, and demonstrated before and since that you are a monster of colossal proportions. Creatures such as yourself are why our kind must live in mystery and secrecy, slinking from sleeping to sleeping, mostly out of the way, instead of helping, where our help is so much needed."

She turned to Stefan. "Who is this man?" she asked him. "Sessai brought you from the Egyptian delta to the Kievan Caves, where you awoke in 1700. He examined the results.." Stefan said glancing at Sessai, "of your handiwork in Kiev and outside Bendery. I pointed you out to him at an intersection not far from here after Poltava."

"My handiwork?" she asked, small tears dripping down her cheeks. "And I don't remember you in Egypt," she said, turning to Sessai.

"You were already boxed when I collected you in Egypt," answered Sessai. "You brutally killed two men in the crypt in Kiev, two others on the road to Bendery, and three soldiers in the Persian Army before leaving to take Charles at Fredrikshald." Sessai was grim.

"Sessai was sent from the head of the order in India to collect you in Egypt," Stefan continued. "Your reputation had already achieved global proportions, even then. Your meddling with Julius and Antony is credited with the end of the Roman Republic and the wars around the ascendency of the first single emperor."

Sessai interjected: "We aren't sure how human history might have progressed without your dramatic involvement then, but the elders are certain the damage you caused physically, and the damage done by the trajectory of human society, are hard to estimate in the full."

"I have worked as an assassin. I can't deny that, and won't. But I believe there was no killing I accepted that wouldn't have been accomplished by some mortal. I just made them… cleaner. And perhaps with lesser fatalities."

"Them?" asked Sessai.

She pondered her options and chose to admit them all. "After Charles, there was Thomas Jackson. Franz Ferdinand. John Bellingham. Vladimir Lenin. George Patton. Bobby Kennedy. Alexander Litvinenko." Her face was morose. "Perhaps I cannot be proud of these, but I wasn't a Hitler henchman, and all would have died, or worse, without my involvement."

Cleo continued, "And Rome? You blame me for Rome? Julius was going to leave it all, to come for me. He knew the risk that March day, but we were so blissful together, our optimism obscured the truth." Tears began in earnest. "They killed him that day, so brutally, so brutally, and all because of me." She turned to Stefan, "He was to me, what your Ukraine wife was to you."

"What you say adds to your crimes. Any excuse is hard to believe, frankly," said Sessai grimly.

"We will convene a trial," added Stefan. She replied to Stefan, "Yes, I was angry at you in Ukraine, for forcing me to marry you. I could have run away.. easily evaded it all. Of course you are aware of this now."

"Yes," nodded Stefan.

"But after I met you, I thought about what I had lost with Julius, and thought, perhaps, I might be able to have a true companion, someone who will join me through eternity. That is why I bit you on our wedding night. Why do you think I was trying to find you, after Poltava? You know I was searching for you, that was why I went to Bendery, and why I enlisted with those Persians."

Stefan and Sessai exchanged glances. "Are you claiming you weren't attempting to make Stefan your vampy?" Sessai asked with a snarl on his lips.

Cleo glanced at Stefan. "I don't know what to say," she replied. Is she feigning sincerity, Stefan wondered.

"Give it some thought. There will be a trial before the council." Sessai secured her chains to the wall. He and Stefan stepped out of the room, then Stefan returned.

"I want to hear it all. For our daughter's sake," he told her. Then he pulled up a chair.

##

The cease fire had been in place for a week. Sessai suggested there were rumors of something more permanent. Olya had described the stand-off in Belorussia, and it appeared that some semblance of a balance of forces made continuation of hostilities "inopportune" for the Russian Republic.

"We interrupt this program to bring you the following important announcement," was the lead-in. After a brief speech from the Russian president, effusive thanks from his Ukraine counterpart, and bear hugs all around, Russian forces left the Donbass and rebels were reintegrated. "Crimea will remain a Russian territory but will be reintegrated with Ukraine in ten years' time," the Russian leader had said.

##

But the kicker, for Vanessa? The day Hank climbed from an Apache at Zaphorizhya International Airport, with her entire troop applauding. That scrawny former Army MP, cum investment banker, got down on his knee and proposed.

How could she say "no?"

Good thing she said "Yes." Unbeknownst to her, Julie had been in country for days planning a simple Russian orthodox wedding. Evidently General Redgrave had arranged transportation from Kansas to Kiev.

There was a beautiful little church in Stary Saltiv. A priest with a colorful sash and lots of incense. Halting English, but who cared about that? The best part of the planning was hugging Julie. Vanessa gazed into her Mom's eyes, contemplating the emotion a mother feels, contemplating how far away Olya was, and how sad that really was, for the two of them.

Vanessa wrapped her arms around Julie. "Thank you so much, Mom." She smiled. "This is one operation I would have had a real hard time planning. But how were you able to do it, not speaking Russian."

"I guess it really wasn't appropriate for Stefan's staff to help. But they did. And believe me, a Deputy from the Rada can certainly pull some weight around here."

Julie smiled. "You must have made quite an impression on that man. He moved mountains for you." Vanessa thought about Stefan. Her father. "If you only knew," she thought. Then she gave Julie another hug.

Will Smith and Stefan Cossack together gave Vanessa away. A brass quintet played "Water Music." Cleo, in chains, sat in the back row, next to Taigen Sessai. Vanessa wasn't sure she had ever seen Hank look so proud. Such wonderful glances at the front of the church.

Such a tender kiss, when the priest granted permission.

At the receiving line, Brig Gen McMaster shook everyone's hand. "Congratulations, Major," was his greeting for Vanessa. "Thanks for arranging the social calendar for the day."

"My pleasure, sir," she blushed.

"I trust you will forgive me for missing the reception." She and Hank responded in unison: "Yes, sir."

There were the Ukrainian folk songs. Country western ballads. Katie Perry pop songs. There was a honeymoon at "Relax," near Poltava, but good bye kisses thereafter. "When will I see him again?" She wondered.

"When will **I see her again?" he wondered. Hank was glad he bought her the ring. A thought worth a smile. At least one.**

##

"Nice tactical operations center," thought General McMaster, as he walked into the fifth floor conference room in a building, in the Northeast Sector of Kharkiv. As the "three" and the "two" scurried around preparing to brief, he marveled at how long it took that star to catch up with him.

It was great to turn the battle space back to the Ukrainian forces. Another National Guard brigade would arrive from the United States next week, to restore a US footprint around Kharkiv. The Second Cav had already been reconstituted. Flattering, they assessed his initial screening positions were still a good starting point.

The 82d Division headquarters would relieve his staff in two months. Redgrave had already gone home. That female air cav troop commander had been one surprise after another. What was her name? Vanessa Smith?

Trans-Siberian

Sessai pulled into the parking lot at the train station. He walked around the car, opened the door for Cleo, then gathered her small bag from the back. They walked toward the station, her trudging and clinking, he deep in thought.

"I have to go to the bathroom," she said. "Fine," was his answer. After some inquiry, they found the ladies room and paid the attendant. His presence was a bit unusual, but the chains were enough of an explanation. He followed her into the stall. "Do you mind?" she asked him, annoyed.

"Take care of business," was his answer. "We have both been through worse."

She dropped her drawers and settled onto the commode, glaring at him. When she was done, she took several sheets of paper, flushed, and restored her clothing. He unlatched the door, motioning for her to exit before him. She walked to the sink and washed her hands.

They trudged to the platform. Platform 10. The train was already waiting. Sessai showed a uniformed train man her ticket, and mentioned in Russian that he was dropping her with another passenger. The train man nodded and they walked aboard.

At the seventh door, Sessai turned the nob. Inside, sitting on the seat, was Stefan. He stood.

Cleo stepped inside the compartment and leaned back against the wall. Sessai handed the key for the chains to Stefan. They exchanged glances. "So you are good here?" Sessai asked.

"We're good," answered Stefan.

Cleo gazed at her East Bank Cossack. Sessai gave his old friend a hug, a glance to his prisoner, and walked to the exit and the platform. "Where to now?" he wondered to himself.

Stefan gazed into the deep brown eyes, the flowing black curls. He realized there was nothing that he wanted more than to unbutton her blouse, cup her breast in his hand, and kiss those bright red lips. Somehow the key in his right hand found its way into the lock, and the chains fell to the ground.

How can a person, or any creature, describe a kiss that has been waiting for centuries? Cleo opened her eyes and caught his quiet soul, gazing back at her. "What to say?" She wondered to herself. Then she thought of something.

"Can we get married?" she asked Stefan.

"I think we already are," he replied, after a brief pause. She wrapped her arms around him and never let go.

The Author

Pete Godston graduated from Johns Hopkins University, where he took one writing seminars course, resolving to live life first, then write later. This is later. Before that class, and since, Pete has been a student of good fiction.

After graduating from Hopkins, Godston served as a Regular Army officer on the Demilitarized Zone in Korea and with the 2d Armored Cavalry Regiment in Germany, ultimately traveling to all continents (except Antarctica). He left active duty to attend Harvard Business School, where he received an MBA in 1989. Since then Pete has gained experience for his fiction from numerous tech, consulting and government contracting firms, but has not made a billion$ in tech or on Wall Street.

Pete continued his military service through the National Guard and Reserves, including leading a battalion-sized task force in Iraq, retiring from the Army Reserves in 2011. He lives near his two daughters in Virginia, where he is working on a big data/cyber security start-up. This is his third book, but his first novel.

Made in the USA
Lexington, KY
29 April 2019